About the author

After failing English Language and English Literature at GCE O level in 1967, the author was apprenticed to a firm of lithographic printers but still maintained an interest in books and writing. A father to two daughters and grandfather to three granddaughters, the author now lives with his partner in Glastonbury and East Anglia.

This, his first novel, was years in the cauldron but now is ready for tasting. He has written several short stories and items of serious and humorous poetry, yet to be published.

BESSOMTHWAITE TWO EIGHT EIGHT

William Buggins

BESSOMTHWAITE TWO EIGHT EIGHT

To Misha,

my best wishes

Wm Buggins

Vanguard Press

A CIP catalogue record for this title is
available from the British Library.

ISBN 978 178 465 198 5

*Vanguard Press is an imprint of
Pegasus Elliot MacKenzie Publishers Ltd.*
www.pegasuspublishers.com

First Published in 2017

**Vanguard Press
Sheraton House Castle Park
Cambridge England**

Printed & Bound in Great Britain

To Mum and Dad, with love and thanks.

Foreword

This, in its entirety, is a work of fiction and nothing more. You may find as my story unfolds names you recognise, places to which you have been, and situations from recent history that ring a bell in your distant memory, but you should consider this to be just a story in the real sense. I do not intend to imply any true reality you may attach to the people, places and times described in this tale.

However, you may well infer, as any discerning reader should, far more than I ever intended to suggest, but this I believe is the essential prerogative of fiction. W.B.

Chapter One

A Speculative Operation

It was barely mid-morning and already the day was getting hot, but General Mahmud Hassan al Majid did not notice this as he stared blankly through the opened window of his office and out past the wide dusty parade ground below. He did not notice the few lethargic soldiers ambling about down there either. Nor did he notice the few remaining old and broken tanks that were left there, parked in the shade and still awaiting repair. Ten years before there would have been a hundred or more, tanks and men, lined up outside his window, all clean and shiny and eager. It was not that he didn't notice these things because he didn't care; quite the contrary. He, like many other Iraqis, was well aware of the deep humiliation they had suffered at the hands of the American led coalition, and he harboured a well hidden but bitter resentment of the situation in which his country had been placed following the Kuwait invasion. Oh he cared all right. He didn't notice those things that day because he was deep in thought.

He sat behind his desk, motionless, feet up, ankles crossed, hands with fingers interwoven clasped behind his head. His large flat topped desk, a sprawl of untidiness, was spread out beneath an ancient air-conditioning unit that dripped water on him from time to time. He had thought about having the unit repaired, but since the unsuccessful Kuwait campaign spare parts of any kind were difficult to find. He had thought about having his desk moved too, so he would not have to sit directly underneath the drip zone, but that would mean losing the view from his first floor window and he did some of his best thinking looking out from that window. Besides, the cool water which anointed him every so often was welcomed and served to cool and refresh him. In the hot, torpid Baghdad afternoons, when he allowed it to trickle down the back of his neck, the cool water would send an enjoyable shiver through him.

Office S.I.9 of the Special Bureau of the Iraqi Intelligence Service, of which General Mahmud was head, was an undesignated section of the important and powerful Directorate 9. In real terms Office S.I.9 was underfunded compared to its bigger brothers such as: Directorate 5, Iraqi Counter Intelligence and the powerful Directorate 14 of the Special Operations Bureau. Although this had never prevented General Mahmud and his team punching well above their weight.

At fifty-seven Mahmud was older than most of the heads of other directorates, and had proven to be a cunning and reliable tactician over the thirty-five years he had been in the service of his country and party. He was neither especially a Ba'athist nor really a devout Muslim, but he was fervently an Iraqi. He studied military history and became addicted to chess when at university and this passion showed in his strategic thinking. He was feared by his equals and those who knew him for the power he wielded, but he was also greatly respected and genuinely revered by his subordinates. Seen as a wise and thoughtful intellectual and a good Muslim, with whom problems could be raised and solved without rage or rancour, there was little those he commanded would not do to earn his praise.

At that precise moment however, he would have appeared to any casual observer to be merely studying his shoes. The old highly polished leather brogues he was wearing rested up against the telephone in front of him. He used to have shoes shipped over from Bond Street, London, before the nastinesses had started and this pair was definitely showing signs of wear, with cracks in the brown leather and holes worn in the soles. His mind though was far away from the condition of his shoes, beyond the open window and the parade ground beneath, beyond even the crushing effects of the UN's punitive sanctions. He was formulating a plan.

A drip that could wait no longer released its grip, fell from the unit above him and splattered on his forehead. The general unfolded his hands and with them wiped the cold water all over his face. It was not enough to properly refresh him but it had broken his concentration finally. He leaned forward with a bit of a struggle and grunted as he did so. He pressed a green button which lit up and activated an intercom on his telephone.

"Come in here a moment, Muhammad, would you?" He spoke towards the phone.

The general pressed the green button again and the light went out. He removed his feet from the desk, lowering the soles of his shoes slowly to the floor and waited for the door to open.

"Sir?" the aide enquired.

"I wish to speak to Mundai at the hotel. Get him to use a secure line," he ordered, gently, "or better still, get him up here."

"Right away, sir," the aide replied and closed the door behind him.

General Mahmud Hassan stood, and opened out the manilla folder on the desk in front of him again. He had walked to the window and back across the room many times that morning with a heavy heart. He crossed the small room once more, and looked out onto the parade ground beyond, but he did so now with the merest hint of a smile on his face and an impish twinkle in his eyes. He turned from the window and looked again at the photograph pinned to the pages in the yellow folder. He stared at the face it showed for some time, in an attempt to gain some intuitive knowledge of the man he was going to try tipping to his own advantage.

"Now we will see how this big fish swims," he said, to no-one in particular. Then he whispered to himself and the picture in front of him, as if in prayer, "Like a salmon I hope, back to the river where you were spawned; perhaps. Taking your country's unholy pollution with you; if I let you, perhaps. And maybe you will help destroy our enemy for us; on a massive scale, perhaps. Allah forgive me. Peace be upon him."

Mundai arrived in the general's office twenty minutes later, hot and breathless.

"Assalamu alaikum, Mundai my dear fellow," (Peace be with you) said the general in greeting.

"Wa alaikum salam," (and peace be unto you) Mundai responded.

"Come, sit. It is a little cooler by the window." The general offered Mundai a seat on the sofa under the opened window but he remained standing with his back to the desk, his arms spread behind him and palms flat on its top.

"Tea?" he asked.

"That would be most welcome on such a hot morning, Shukran, General," Mundai replied, respectfully accepting the general's hospitality.

The general turned and pressed the green button twice and spoke into the telephone.

"Is there chai in the samovar, Muhammad? Yes please. No, just fill two glasses and bring them if you would. Leave whatever you are doing," he instructed, and pressed the green button once more so the briefing would remain private.

"Your family, they are well?" the general enquired.

"They are all blossoming, General. I have three girls, you remember?" asked Mundai. "My father looks after them, since my wife was killed in the bombing."

"Yes, I do remember, now you mention it. Truly unfortunate," the general remarked. To have no sons and no wife he felt was a double blow. "You must take another wife, soon, Mundai, and perhaps then you'll have sons to assist you."

"If Allah wishes it will be so, yes," Mundai agreed, rather embarrassed that this meeting had momentarily become so personal. What was it the general really wanted of him?

"Your father, yes, I am interested in him too, and he still owes me a favour. He will be perfect for what I have in mind. I will telephone him when we have finished."

Tea arrived and, at the general's request, Muhammad placed the silver tray on a small low table beside the large sofa where Mundai was sitting. Filled with steaming hot chai, each glass stood on a silver saucer in an ornate silver holder that had two beautiful swan's neck handles and a tiny silver spoon beside it. When his aide had left the room General Mahmud sat down next to Mundai on the sofa and handed one of the glasses carefully to him. Mundai stirred in the sugar at the bottom of his glass and took a sip of the strong, sweet, cardamom flavoured beverage.

"It is to your liking?" the general asked politely.

"Yes, shukran," Mundai replied. "I find it most refreshing, sir."

General Mahmud reached over and picked up the manilla folder he had placed on the table before Mundai arrived.

"This is the man you have requested travel and access permits for. Read the dossier."

While Mundai was reading the general stood up again and went to his desk. From a drawer he brought out two pink forms and a plastic card.

"I apologise, sir, I had no idea. All his paperwork says weapons inspector."

"Don't apologise, my friend, we all must wear many hats in this life. His guardian is an old friend of mine from before the war. As you can see from the file Eric Lomas is British Secret Service but our intelligence shows he has not been operational for over six months. I believe he is here, genuinely, to see the final resting place of his beloved family, but as he is here officially to find weapons of mass destruction, I think we ought to let him find some." The general handed the travel permits and the security pass to Mundai and sat down in the chair opposite him.

"But what good would this do? I thought we were trying to hide WMDs from the UN inspectors." Mundai was more than a little surprised.

"The truth is we don't really have that many left to hide, at least not of our own making. This doesn't mean we can't make mischief with the few we have left though, does it? The WMDs were always more of a myth cooked up by his highness to scare the West. Our nuclear capability was never intended to be anything other than peaceful, but then the Israelis blew up the reactor at Osirak in 1981 and he went mad. He wanted superguns built, long range rockets to deliver sarin and anthrax to Jerusalem. So now we are in Jihad; a holy war against the

Great Satan that is the whole of western civilization." General Mahmud Hassan was warming to his subject now.

He continued, "We may be at war against the Great Satan, but does he come and fight? No! We are at war and we have to go and fight him. We blow up his embassies or damage some of his shipping. That is like having a peashooter in a playground to him. We are never going to make any serious impact unless we draw them into us. This was the underlying purpose behind the Kuwait war, well that and the acquisition of the oil fields and the seaport terminals. No, Saddam wanted most of all to draw the West into a war they could not win, on our territory, here in Iraq. What stopped them?"

"They had no UN mandate to invade Iraq, only to liberate Kuwait," Mundai proffered.

"Exactly, so everything is on hold for now. Al Qaeda has a scheme to bring down the World Trade Centre towers, but I don't see that taking off; they've tried several time before and failed. So I am thinking we must give the Americans a reason to come for us. We must give them a reason to believe they need to fight a war here and in doing so we are going to help them get the UN resolution they require. Then they will come, and the streets of Baghdad will run red with the blood of the Infidel. Allah forgive me, peace be upon him."

Mundai swallowed a little more of his tea, wondering how he was to be implicated in this. He was about to find out.

The general took two deep gulps from his glass and set it down empty on the tray emphatically. His mouth had become dry from his excited outburst, now his throat was slaked he stood and resumed.

"I want you to take him, with the others, this afternoon. I have arranged the transportation. A bus will be at the hotel at noon, two of our brothers from Directorate 5 will already be aboard to ensure you have no trouble with him. They will not get in your way, but they are good men so you will be in no danger. The hotel manager will be informed that you must escort our guests, so you will have no problems from him fulfilling your obligations to me. Understand?"

"Understood," Mundai confirmed with a confidence that belied his underlying feeling of panic at the mention of the word danger. He was not a soldier, just a supplier of information on any of his hotel's foreign guests. He also worried what he would do with his daughters now his father was going to be involved in the scheme. His late wife's sister would have to have them, pick them up from school.

"I do not want Mr Lomas hindered in any way, especially at the Razazah compound. A small amount of Bessomthwaite 288, the bio-agent that killed his family at Karbala, has been stored in Al-Razazah since the clean-up operation. The area is safe now, but it is this I wish Lomas to find. Do you have any questions, Mundai?"

Mundai thought over the plot and its purpose. He saw many flaws, which he was not prepared to begin to explore with his superior, but decided to question something at least.

"Will not the British deny the existence of such material here and it's supply, by them, for us to use against the Iranians all those years ago?" he asked, hesitantly.

"That is a good question. What will they do? I have no real way of knowing. However, my intention is to place the British government in a situation where they can no longer deny its existence and are compelled to join the Americans and attack Iraq. Once Lomas leaves Iraqi territory with some of it who knows what he might do with it. In the event we wait for a large or limited return on our investment. This is a speculative operation that requires patience and patience is a virtue I have in abundance, my dear Mundai."

General Mahmud went over to his desk again and from a drawer took out a small maroon booklet with the coat of arms of the British Royal Family embossed on its cover.

"Give him his passport back along with these other documents before he leaves the hotel for Al-Razazah." The general placed the two pink slips and the plastic card inside the passport and handed it to Mundai. "The sooner he chooses to leave Baghdad after your trip the better. There is a plane to Paris at midnight, the French nurse is booked on it, and I have made arrangements for a seat to be reserved for any last minute traveller who may wish to leave with her. Let us hope he chooses to do so."

Mundai suddenly realised the briefing was over. He hurriedly drained his glass, and stood up.

"No slip ups." The general's words followed Mundai to the door.

"No, sir," he assured him, as he shut door.

Mundai hurried away muttering, "No slip ups, definitely no slip ups." He knew the penalty for slip ups. His own father was a constant reminder of what can happen to anyone in Iraq who 'slips up'. He had once been high in the internal security service of Iraq and a special guard of the President, Saddam Hussein himself. But something happened and his father was instantly stripped of his position and power and left to live as other Iraqis who have no wealth or influence.

Mundai knew he and his father would not be back from Karbala before nightfall and there was a lot to do. Everything else he was fine with. He was even coming to terms with the danger and to be honest he was a little excited at the prospect of being in harm's way for once, but he had to ensure the girls were looked after. He needed to telephone Nadia for the children's pick-up from school and it was not a call he looked forward to making with any relish. His superior, the general, could be a fearsome man when things failed to fall into place, but seldom produced anything like the wrath his sister-in-law could when she was put out.

Chapter Two

A Weapon of Mass Destruction

Anthrax; sounds lethal does it not? The word alone embodies fears resting deep within us. The very idea of anthrax evokes the terror of plagues and pestilences too devastating for mankind to overcome, of overwhelming natural disasters of biblical proportions sent by an angry and vengeful God. Yet in its simplest form anthrax occurs naturally on the hides of our domestic cattle as spores and very seldom adversely affects the creatures with which it naturally comes into contact.

In the late nineteen fifties, research was secretly resumed into bio-chemical weapons as a more manageable alternative to the environmentally dirty and structurally devastating A and H bombs. Several small unobtrusive laboratories were set up in low density population areas, tucked away, out of sight around the country. The laboratory in the north west of England which was given anthrax to develop became known as Bessomthwaite 288: the telephone number it was first ascribed. And so the lethal pathogen Bessomthwaite 288, a derivative of modified anthrax, took its name from a small post-war research unit where it was first refined and then perfected, following a fatal accident in 1972 in the primate laboratory.

A monkey was being prepared for tests using an, as yet, untested strain of anthrax serum. The monkey wriggled and a small amount of the serum was injected into the assisting micro-biologist who was holding the small primate. As soon as this refined anthrax came in contact with the human immune system, it developed the ability to mutate and formed a new pathogen which could hide itself by disguising itself as a micro-organism which a human's immune system would not recognise as hostile or toxic. It was found later that only humans seem to be affected by this. The monkey received his injection in the end, but survived.

The assistant, however, died a horribly slow death from internal bleeding, surviving for over two weeks. Her husband, who had administered the fatal dose, kept notes, at her request, documenting her deterioration for research purposes. Every drop of her blood was vacuumed up and stored for future analysis and development. It was very quickly developed into an airborne pathogen able to survive for long periods outside the body before entering other hosts and overwhelming them too. Bessomthwaite 288 was created from a single bag of her blood and then refined into the most potentially lethal substance known to mankind at the time. In the secret world of bio-weaponry, the technicians at Bessomthwaite were hailed as heroes for their world beating scientific breakthrough. They had discovered the perfect biological weapon.

Eventually the unfortunate but brave bio-chemist died, her body incinerated and her ashes placed in a lead lined box. Her grave is in a small cemetery near Bessomthwaite, where an unobtrusive headstone bears her name and a coffin is buried. However, what happened to the lead lined box is not known and there is no mention of her ultimate sacrifice to the advancement of biological science on that headstone. The assistant's name was Ilyana Lomas, née Kadich and she is a very important part of this story.

Certainly her son, Eric Lomas, would not have argued the point. Nearly thirty years after his mother's tragic death, he found himself on a sun bed beside the pool of a Baghdad hotel waiting for the papers required to visit a war grave containing all of his own young family. Ten years after the end of the first Gulf war, mystery still surrounded the deaths of his wife and two sons. Lack of information and access for relatives once the names of the victims were finally released had aroused Lomas's suspicions that the true nature of their deaths had been concealed. He had not considered the possibility of there being any similarity between their deaths and that of his mother.

Surrounded by the constant clicking and fizzing of crickets, which he fancied sounded like high voltage electricity passing through low density cables, he lay stretched out on the apron of the hotel's outdoor pool, drowsing under a wide parasol which shaded the whole of him from the whole of the mid-morning sun. The hotel in which he was staying was, naturally, one of Baghdad's finest. The British taxpayer always provided their top agents with first-class facilities. He laughed to himself at this thought, particularly as he was paying for this jaunt himself. Unused to this level of inactivity his mind started to wandered into territory it seldom visited, remembering some of the old missions, remembering some of the dreadful places he had slept and worked when he had been fully operational. The night, for instance, he had spent in a mass grave with the bodies of children and women killed in Sarajevo thrown over him in order to keep himself hidden from the Serb gunmen pursuing him: that had been rather a low point he felt. Or the afternoon he got really drunk in Gibraltar with three IRA suspects. They had no idea he was an Englishman, let alone Special Service. Unfortunately neither did the SAS. team that shot them down in the street outside the bar which he and the suspects had just left. How they had not killed him was just lucky. He was shot in the thigh on that occasion, but was able to testify at the ensuing enquiry later that the SAS. men had indeed issued a warning and that the Irishmen were all carrying hand guns and some amounts of high explosive. He never did get to properly thank the guys at Hereford, he now remembered, for that extended stay in hospital, however apologetic they had been. They admitted only his appearance as a smelly drunken Spaniard had stopped them from blowing his head off. He remembered how the stench of his own body and clothes had made him retch but how after a day or two he had gotten used to the odour. But he could never get used to waking up with a hangover; he had hated that.

Even in the shade of the bright yellow canvas of his parasol, Lomas was hot. He liked to be hot, to feel hot, in the same way he liked to be cold, to feel cold. Being warm, like being chilly, only annoyed him. He'd had little time for the ordinary in life. In ordinary conditions you feel very little. Life is different lived at extremes. Makes you certain you are alive. It was in spite of this he had placed himself in the shade, and been pleasantly surprised to find the heat there still overpowering. He was not interested in getting a tan, and the Arabian sun burned those who did not respect its power. There were some around the pool this morning he noticed, who would suffer later that evening and for days to come. From the broad shadow in which he was laying and with his eyes behind dark glasses, the precise direction of his gaze was hidden. He could survey the other guests at his leisure as they jockeyed for their favourite sunspots or found places with friends, unaware he was anything other than asleep. He had discovered, with a deal of satisfaction, that by speculating on the nature of people before he actually met them, he was generally good at reading people. Practice in any skill was never time wasted. This was how he intended to spend his first full day in Iraq; people watching.

Having arrived the previous evening from Paris, and although he had registered his request immediately when he checked-in, he calculated that the papers and permits required for him to visit the graves would take several days to arrive. He was in no hurry to start this final part of his repair process. He had been happier lately, in his grief, than he'd been for the past ten years, although it had kept him sharp and focused on his work, and his work had allowed him little time to dwell on situations he could not change. He had come to Iraq to say goodbye to them, not goodbye from him, but to let them go, as much as anything. He knew he would still hear a young boy's voice calling 'Dad' in the street, and turn to answer thinking it was either Luke or Mikey. He still would catch the faint scent of spring hyacinths and think of her, his lovely Katherine; her face before him long after the mild perfume had drifted away on the breeze. He smiled at the thought of it. He smiled at the thought of her.

Once, not long after they were married, she had written him a note and slipped it in with his passport. He was being sent out again to limit the fallout from the messy situation that had occurred in Gibraltar that spring. At passport control a piece of coloured notepaper had fallen out from the leaves of the thin blue book. The paper was impregnated with a pungent scent that reminded him at the time of hyacinths and on the paper she had written a short poem.

When the days paint grey on greys
and rain comes again
to drown the green ground,
a memory of your face
will easily replace
the sun for me.

He had carried it with him ever since: the note and the
sentiment.

From his vantage point in the shade he watched the others
around the pool amble listlessly towards noon. He had spotted
no-one that particularly tweaked his interest. There were a few
couples, mainly wealthy Iraqis weekending, and a large group
of noisy, vociferous Italians on holiday. There was another
lone male sitting at a table away from the noisy group. He had
white spindly legs that dangled from wide dark blue shorts, his
feet barely reaching the floor. Banker, Lomas thought, German
banker. He had overheard him order a cold beer from one of
the pool waiters, who floated like wraiths between the tables
and the sunbeds doing their best to stay out of the sun. The
German was wearing dark glasses and like Lomas was
probably people watching too, except it was fairly obvious that
this little German had a fascination for large married Iraqi
women.

Lomas turned his attention to the lone young woman who
had occupied the shade two rows away from his. Even before
he heard her speak he had guessed she was French. French
women have a certain *je ne c'est quoi*! He watched her
preparations to take a swim. She removed her sandals showing
that her toe and finger nails were immaculately painted with a
dark crimson varnish. She had strong shapely legs and a rather
pretty face with little cosmetic, if any. Her skin looked silky

and lightly tanned already. When she removed her top and shorts she revealed a red and black 'V' striped bikini; and the fact that she looked after herself. Her ample breasts were an exuberant filling for the bikini top, and he noticed her firm buttocks tighten when she dipped one foot into the cool water of the pool.

As he watched this nymph descend gracefully into the water, he saw that the diminutive German banker had shifted his gaze too. He was looking straight at Lomas, and was writing something in a thin notebook on the table beside him. Lomas made a note too; the banker was left handed.

The girl swam well. Her cropped brown hair laying flat in curls across the nape of her neck showed her ears, pierced and studded with a single white stone, each one like a gleaming pearl in an open shell. The banker had shifted his attentions back to the large Iraqi women, but Lomas remained with the swimmer and admired her long, languid style of stroke. After a time she cruised to the side and lifted herself out onto the hot stone flags that edged the pool. She pulled up with her a great quantity of water; like a big fish does when it rises clear of the surface. She was shining and brilliant as a hooked tuna tossed into a boat. Her glistening breasts still rising and falling from the exercise she rested there for a moment, regaining her breath. Water cascaded from her sparkling body into a dark spreading puddle on the bleached stone tiles around her. She pulled her legs up into her chest and stood up. The muscles of her thighs were the gleaming flanks of wet dolphins that caught the sunlight as they flexed.

Lomas began to feel the faint beating of a long forgotten drum thump again deep within him. It had been over ten years since he had felt excitement towards a woman, for a woman, and it was not something he had expected or necessarily wanted, but there it was just the same and becoming just as insistent as it had been before, rising like a salacious phoenix through the grim reality of his situation and reasons for being in Baghdad. Right now he needed to be focused.

Lomas looked away quickly, slightly annoyed with himself and his feelings. The little German banker was looking straight at him again, and Lomas's embarrassment suddenly transformed into anger and hostility. He decided he would need to revise his initial thoughts about Herr Notebook. He lay back on the bed and closed his eyes. He tried to bring Katherine's face to mind and when he had done so the violent turmoil within him had subsided and he was smiling to himself and he was sunny again. "Ah, I've got it," he said to himself. "Reporter. He's not a banker, he's a reporter."

He lay there for some time with his eyes shut and when he opened them again and sat up on his elbow to scan the pool once more, the French woman and the German reporter were gone.

Mundai Sabawi al Tikriti was sitting in the shade of the great awning at the pool bar talking to a pool waiter, but when he spotted Lomas sitting up, under his shade, Mundai walked over to him hurriedly and greeted him.

The exact definition of Mundai's employment at the hotel was unknown to all but two people; neither of them was Mundai himself. The owner of the hotel who paid his embarrassingly large salary was one. Mundai however was expected to carry out any duties the owner saw fit to allocate to him. He could serve at the bar; he could wait at the tables in the fine dining salon, croupier in the casino, and in fact filled any gaps that occasionally appeared in the famously outstanding service the hotel's guests expected. He spoke five European languages including Greek and several other Arabic dialects as well as his own. Besides the owner, he was his own boss in the hotel and carried an authority that was never challenged by any of the other hotel staff, even the irascible and pompous manager, Maurice le Clare.

Given his command of so many foreign tongues Mundai found the position of customer liaison fell naturally to him, much to the visible annoyance of the gregarious Maurice. Mundai greeted the guests on arrival, and if they had any problems he was there to solve them with as little fuss as possible. This intimacy with the guests enabled him to fulfil his duty to his primary employer. It was this work Mundai took very seriously. So it was as the hotel's 'meeter and greeter' that Mundai had welcomed Eric Lomas on his arrival.

Even though it had been late the previous evening when Lomas arrived, Mundai considered it vital the general should know at once that a British Inspector of Weapons had checked in wanting papers for al-Razazah.

"Hello again, Mr Lomas. I thought you were asleep."

"Just resting my eyes, Mundai my dear fellow," he replied.

"I have your papers here for al-Razazah and security pass, all authorized at the highest level. Oh, and here is your passport."

"I am impressed. I thought it would take some time to get through the departments."

"You have been lucky, if lucky is the right word in these circumstances. There are others going today at noon by special bus to Karbala and Bahr al-Mihl: that is Lake Razazah, where the cemetery has been made. There are a couple from this hotel going out there too, so it was rushed through. Can you be ready in time?" Mundai asked, but then wished he had insisted on it. His arrangements were centred round Lomas.

"I can be ready in thirty minutes. I just need to shower and change into appropriate clothing. I'll be in reception at noon."

"Thank you, Mr Lomas. If it is going to be the driver I think taking us, he is a bad tempered so and so and he won't wait for anyone," said Mundai, somewhat relieved.

Mundai thanked Lomas again and scurried off. He reminded himself that this was the general's plan, a general who insisted there be no slip-ups. This thought, and standing in full sun as he had been, made Mundai hot and more than a little panicky, he needed a shower and a long cool drink of tea before noon arrived. Firstly though he needed to call Nadia, his sister-in-law, and persuade her to collect his children from school, only then could he properly cool down and calm himself before the afternoon's journey into the desert.

Chapter Three

The Road to Razazah

Lomas was last to join the small bus in which they were to travel. There were several other occupants besides Mundai's little group, but it was far from full. He walked slowly down the central aisle towards the middle seats where Mundai was perched. He nodded to the other occupants as he passed and they nodded back with a kind of grim recognition. There was an Iraqi family of five, silent in grief, the husband with his arm around his wife consoling her. They were smartly dressed in western clothes, their shoes unavoidably dusty. There were two elderly couples, Arabs with no children any more, both women sobbing quietly. Lomas went and sat with Mundai half-way down the bus. Mundai was with two others from the hotel: the German reporter and the French woman he had seen earlier by the pool. Two men in traditional Arab dress sat at the back of the bus, on their own. They watched Lomas as he took a seat across the aisle from Mundai. Lomas saw they had guns concealed beneath their *dishdashahs* and guessed they were state security. The bus and its driver coughed and spluttered into life and they headed off through the bombed-out suburbs of Baghdad, along the main southern highway.

The road out of Baghdad was a wide dual carriageway and hard topped, but there were many places where large areas of its surface had been filled in with just dirt and bricks, in an attempt to flatten out the craters caused by coalition bombing. Their driver, a bad tempered Arab, who Mundai referred to as

Khalid, was giving a running commentary in Arabic between coughing fits as he drove them at a demonic pace out of the city. He had an old face, unshaven and the few teeth he had left in his mouth were brown and crooked. Lomas noticed, when boarding the bus, Khalid was not wearing shoes just a dirty pair of old flip-flops. He also sported a grubby red and white chequered *shumagg* with a frayed black *ogal* holding it in place on his head, and like his stained and dusty *dishdashah,* this head scarf had seen better days. There was no doubting Khalid had too, and he was not afraid to let as many foreigners as he could know that this was so. Waving his arms this way and that to emphasise his obvious frustration at having to drive anywhere in the afternoon heat, Khalid seemed to have little to no regard for the comfort of his passengers. He appeared more intent on avoiding every single unfilled pot-hole in the road. This he managed by suddenly grabbing the steering-wheel with both hands and jerking the wheel violently from left to right, and then from right to left again. These manoeuvres were always followed up with another torrent of Arabic abuse.

He continued his tirade as the bus careered its way beyond the Tigris bridges and out into the less densely populated dusty interior of Iraq, towards the Euphrates and the crossing at Al Musayyib. On either side of the road, which had now become little more than a single lane dirt track, small clusters of tanks and lorries left burned out and rusting served as a grim reminder of the Desert Storm operations. They passed small groups of people walking on the road, and a number of high flat-topped carts, heavily laden usually with what seemed to be the total contents of someone's house. These rusty old trailers with their thick lorry tyred wheels were slowly pulled along, invariably by unhappy, malnourished donkeys that forced Khalid to slacken the pace momentarily or run them down. He would wait for the oncoming traffic to disperse and part a little before taking an exaggeratedly wide course around them and shout to each cart driver in turn an extended string of Arabian insults, followed up every time, in English, by: "God damned Bedouin; should stay in the desert!" Then he'd laugh to himself at this, and fall silent again.

These episodes became less frequent as the bus left the city further behind. Khalid's driving settled into a kind of frantic rhythm they could all cope with and an uneasy peace descended on the travellers as the bus sped along the desert road south, followed by its own vapour trail of dust and sand.

Mundai decided to introduce Lomas to the other two travellers from the hotel: the German note taker and the pretty French woman from the poolside.

"We are all here for the same purposes," he began. "The burial sites are west of the lake at Razazah. The journey is about ninety minutes usually, but the way Khalid is driving this afternoon possibly less. Karbala compound is just eighty kilometres but the Christian burial site is further on at Bahr al Mihl, beside the lake there. You must each of you have questions about the fashion in which this sad event was handled by our authorities, but I am afraid I can tell you very little."

"I have indeed many questions, *effendi*, the first of which being why has it taken all this time to allow relatives to visit the graves?" It was the German note taker, Herr Notebook. "There are many of my countrymen killed here and their families have a right to know what happened to them"

"All in good time, Herr Metzer, all in good time," Mundai replied calmly. "I should first introduce you to one another."

Metzer interrupted him and took over, "I am Günter, Günter Metzer, foreign correspondent for the newspaper Hamburger Zeitung. I am making compassionate report to the paper of the delay in allowing access to these areas to the relatives of the victims."

So, Lomas had been right in the end, not a German banker then, as he had first thought. He noticed though that Günter's German accent sounded slightly more American suddenly. He had obviously learned his English in the States or from Americans. He offered his hand and the German took it and shook it, hard. Lomas felt the hard calluses running along the lower edge of Metzer's palm and recognised them for what they were. His own hands also displayed these consequences of tough martial art training. Herr Metzer was not just an ordinary journalist either.

"And you are Eric Lomas, a member of the UN weapons inspection team, whose wife and twin sons were killed in Karbala by coalition bombing, and are here to visit their graves for the first time in ten years; as are we all." Lomas was beginning to develop an intense dislike for Herr Metzer and it showed in the silence that followed.

"I am a journalist, I have to be thorough," Metzer explained.

"Quite so, thank you, Günter. Our lady companion is Fabien Neuville," Mundai said quickly. "I believe it was your brother who perished at Karbala?"

"Oui," was all the French swimmer was prepared to say. Lomas noticed a Parisian accent and her shyness. He also noticed his inner drum take up the beat again.

Metzer jumped in yet again. "Francoise Neuville, petro-chemicals expert working for the Kuwait National Petroleum Company as a technical advisor in the Al Wafra oilfields."

Metzer rattled off the facts as tactfully as if it were a school oral test. "Kidnapped by the retreating Iraqis, and brought to Karbala following Saddam's order to burn the wells when the Americans launched their offensive to regain Kuwait. He has not been heard of since, until this last month. It was always assumed that he, along with others captives were being used as human shields to deflect coalition bombing from vital military sites and now it appears to be so. Well that worked didn't it? He was blown to hell along with the rest of them." He stretched out a hand towards the others in the bus.

"He was my brother," whispered Fabien. She struggled to hold back her tears.

"Hey, Metzer, hold on here, there's no need for all this candour, old boy. Save your spiel for your readers, there are people hurting here, myself included." Lomas's pain and anger was sudden and plain for all to see. He handed Fabien his white handkerchief to dry her eyes.

"Of course, I am sorry, I forget sometime how hurtful what I write can be when it is spoken. I apologise without reservation. It was insensitive of me." Metzer saw then, in the intensity of his expression, the anger Lomas was directing towards him. "You don't like me very much, do you?"

"I don't like anyone very much. Don't think you are anything special." Lomas replied.

"I still can't understand why it has taken ten years to release any sort of statement about this one particular site. All the others were emblazoned over the world's media. Could it have been a nuclear accident, which would explain your presence here, Mr Lomas. Looking for weapons of mass destruction are we?" Günter Metzer persisted, fencing with Lomas.

"Apparently there are none to be found," Lomas parried.

"That doesn't mean there aren't any though, does it?"

"Indeed. They seem to have disappeared, along with your German accent." Touché to Lomas.

Metzer flushed slightly but remained silent. He knew now this Lomas was no blunt instrument.

Scrubland and open desert flashed by in a monotonous blur. Eventually they crossed a newly constructed road bridge that spanned the wide muddy waters of the river Euphrates. Not long after, the bus approached and passed through the town of Karbala. A large expanse of water came into view beyond the road to their right, which Lomas guessed was Lake Razazah. They were out in desert scrub again and the further they drove the more remote they seemed to be from any form of urbanization or even signs of a bedouin population.

The sandy dunes of the open desert had given way to tundra that was more compact and stable. Here, behind a high fence that enclosed an area the size of at least two soccer pitches were three high mounds of naked earth. Atop each one was a large white cross and small concrete obelisk which bore the names of those buried beneath. There was a guard post at the gate and two other low buildings inside the compound between the mounds.

The barrier was lifted as the bus approached the guard post. It appears we are expected, Lomas thought.

The burial mounds were about ten feet high and a flight of white painted steps with a handrail each side rose to a fenced area which surrounded each white cross and obelisk. A set of steps descending down the far side meant that mourners could stand and read the names they wanted to find then move on, without having to turn and face the next group coming up behind them. There were no other mourners that afternoon. When the bus came to an abrupt stop with Khalid's unsympathetic application of the brakes, a civilian Iraqi woman from one of the administration buildings came and asked them to leave the bus and line up to be searched. She directed the Iraqis and the other Christian Arabs away from the bus to the nearest mound to pay their respects and honour their dead. Fabien and Metzer, after a perfunctory search, were escorted to the central grave site and they ascended the steps together. The two men in the back seats with the guns up their shirts stayed in the coach and smoked and exhibited a total disregard for the solemnity of the proceedings. Khalid appeared to have fallen asleep over the steering wheel in the short space of time it had taken the others to leave the bus.

Mundai stood with Lomas whilst he was being thoroughly searched by one of the military personnel guarding the complex.

"No photography allowed here," barked the guard as he examined Lomas's small camera. He seemed otherwise satisfied that Lomas presented no threat to the security of the cemetery.

"I'll remember that," Lomas replied. As the guard handed it back to him, Lomas switched on the tiny Geiger counter the camera contained. It made no noise but a small light would flash if there was a higher than normal level of radiation in the area. No light appeared. He switched it off.

"Just go up those white steps," Mundai advised. "There are steps on the other side and a path that will lead you to the visitor centre, where you can get water and food should you require it. We will be here for an hour at least so take all the time you need. I'll be in the visitor centre should you need any assistance."

"Thank you, Mundai. I had no idea how hard this was going to be."

"I am sure. My sympathies, if this is not inappropriate?"

"Not at all, Mundai, you are a kind man."

Lomas scaled the steps to the rostrum above the furthest mound. He was quite alone. He read the words on the plaque, and saw the names of his Katherine and his two sons. It was hard for him to stand there, not feeling anything. The scars he had healed years ago, and there was nothing left there but a hole that had been part of his life. He felt guilty feeling this way but one had to carry on. He had little time for sentiment in his life. From a young age he had known tragedy and saw how life carried on around him regardless of his feelings. He just felt hollow somehow. He turned and descended the steps to the path below. On reaching the last step, from behind him a voice spoke.

"Follow me. I have something to show you," the voice insisted in a harsh whisper. It was a voice he recognised from the bus. "Come, this way."

It was Khalid that led him to a corrugated-iron shack behind the nearest of the two reception buildings. The shack had no windows and the small narrow door at the side seemed to be the only entrance. Looking over his shoulder Khalid fiddled in the keyhole of the lock with a piece of thin wire he had concealed in the folds of his *shumagg*.

"Are you any good with locks? Look at what they give me to work with," Khalid cursed. He held out the piece of wire to Lomas.

"I'm not sure I want to get involved in this."

"Listen, I hate these bastards as much as you do. I was once an important man in Baghdad. Saddam took everything I had and banished me from the city like a common peasant. Now I am a big man in the resistance against him. In here is what killed your family. In here is what is left of Saddam's chemical weapon capability. You don't want to get involved; you are involved, personally and professionally. I know you are weapons inspector and not just a grieving husband. Now are you going to open this damned door or not?"

"Give it to me," Lomas replied, looking straight into Khalid's tired, sloughed eyes.

Inside were stacks of boxes covered over with tarpaulins. There were some rusting drums with thick red non-viscous fluid bleeding from their seams.

"This all should have been buried years ago. All this stuff looks old to me," said Lomas.

"It is some of what was left after the war with Iran. I was one of the drivers that brought it here. I could not get other work at the time. But most here come from the ruins of the Karbala compound. It is why this area has been restricted for so long. Until recently it has been too toxic." Khalid watched for a reaction from Lomas. There was none.

"The terrible things we do to each other, these people are evil," he added. "You must tell your people of your discovery without alerting Saddam's special police. The two at the back of the coach are ISP: Iraqi Security Police," Khalid explained.

"I thought they might be," said Lomas.

He had pulled back a dusty tarpaulin which covered a small group of canisters. They showed several logos and warnings of hazardous waste and flammability, but there emblazoned on the lids of the eight canisters was the unmistakable telltale stamp of origin; Bsthwt 288. He began carefully to peel back the lid of the topmost canister. Then he was tearing frantically at it as the full force of his rage took hold.

"No! No! No-o-o-!" howled Lomas. "Not like that, not by this, this, not this. No!" His voice trailed off into silence as he imagined the horror of how his family must have died – his sons, his beautiful wife.

"Keep your voice down, you'll bring the guards on us." Khalid was genuinely concerned and backed away towards the open door.

Inside the canister were very many separate sealed gloves of polystyrene. Lomas removed one and split it open. Lomas slid out two small vials which contained a bright magenta liquid.

"What are you doing?" Khalid was outside the shed and peering in from a safe distance.

"Removing evidence," Lomas replied. He stood, not moving, holding the tubes of pink liquid up to the light, stunned by disbelief. He felt another wave of anger welling up inside him as he put together the pattern of events that must inevitably have taken place to so horrifically end the lives of his entire family.

"You'll kill us all you fool. Just take some pictures with that camera of yours; they never check you on the way out." Khalid was quite panic stricken. This was not part of his plan.

"Can't risk it. Don't worry I have an idea," said Lomas, calmer now. Making least fuss was what he did best. He had to get clear, to somewhere safe where he could think this whole thing through.

He pressed the seal of the partially empty glove back together, slotted it into its place with the others and carefully replaced the lid of the canister.

"There, nobody would ever guess we've been," he said, as he pulled the tarpaulin back over the eight canisters and brushed the dust from his trousers.

"But you can't just walk around with them in your pocket, you could wipe out everyone on the bus," Khalid implored.

"It's best then you don't know where they are, but they will be safe don't you worry. I know a place I can take them."

Lomas had the sketch of a plan drawing itself in his quick and lethal mind. This will impress the hell out of my father, he was thinking as he closed and relocked the metal door of the shack. Not many people get to surprise Sir Geoffrey. That bastard lied to me, Lomas was thinking, he told me it had all been destroyed after my mother's death.

Khalid wanted to be off and away back to the bus. Lomas thanked him for risking so much and assured him of the importance of this find.

"I risk nothing, I have nothing to lose. I am only a poor bedouin who wants to see his country free again."

"This discovery will bring us into the war that the Americans want. Britain has always resisted another war but it will be hard for them to find adequate excuses not to commit to war and regime change if this is placed into the hands of the right people," replied Lomas.

"You are a great man, sahib, but may Allah protect you and those little tubes." And he was gone.

Lomas found Mundai in the visitor centre sitting on his own drinking a glass of hot tea. One of the Arab families sat some distance away in a huddle of grief so Lomas asked Mundai if he could sit with him. He too ordered hot tea and they both sat sipping their teas quietly, not speaking.

It struck Lomas that Bessomthwaite 288 must be very powerful stuff for it to be used in such small quantities. How was he going to get the two vials out of the country undetected? He would need a different passport if he did not want to waste time and go overland. He would need to become less conspicuous if the airport was going to be his choice. One man travelling alone always attracts attention. But firstly he needed to dispose of two AAA batteries. Needed only to power the flash of his camera, he had removed them to make room for the two magenta vials filled with death and disease.

He got up from his seat and walked slowly over to a vending machine by the information desk and bought a can of cola.

"That will not refresh you like the tea does," advised Mundai when Lomas sat down again.

"Habit."

"I see. Yet you strike me as a person above habit," Mundai observed.

Lomas opened the can and took a sip.

"It's the caffeine I'm afraid."

"Ahh."

Mundai returned his attention to the other mourners beginning to assemble around their bus and he did not see Lomas slip the two AAA batteries from a pocket in his shirt into the can of cola. Mundai stood and spoke in Arabic to the family in the corner. They stood and walked out.

"Time to go, Mr Lomas, are you ready?"

"As I'll ever be." Lomas took one more careful sip of his cola before he dropped the can into the flip top bin by the exit as he left.

Once again Lomas was the only passenger to be thoroughly searched before boarding, despite Khalid's assurances. He was glad he had disposed of the batteries; they would have provoked some suspicions and unwanted attention from the guards if they had found them. He was about to step onto the bus when one of the security men, with the guns stuffed under their shirts from the back of the bus, blocked his way.

"Step back. I must check your camera. Give it to me please," he insisted.

Lomas stepped back and handed the camera to him obediently. The atmosphere had suddenly become very tense. The security official took the camera over to the uniformed guard who had searched all the passengers. The security man spoke quietly to the guard so Lomas could not hear what was said, but the guard suddenly snapped to attention and flushed deeply as though he had been severely reprimanded. The security officer returned slowly to confront Lomas, tossing the camera from hand to hand as he scrutinised its every detail. The tension was mounting, noticeably.

"He has a permit for the camera," explained Mundai, hoping to defuse a situation he could see developing.

"He may have a permit for the camera but does he have a permit for the film inside it?" It was obvious to all present the official did not expect an answer and none was forthcoming. "I think not," he concluded.

Mundai was growing fearful now of how Lomas would react. He knew of what Eric Lomas was capable and braced himself for an impending fire storm of action. The tension was becoming noticeable even to all those watching this charade from inside the bus. Lomas concealed his own anxiety as best he could but it was he and he alone who knew the certain consequences of even the slightest mishap now.

However, the intense interest shown by the security officer when he first inspected the camera had already turned to distain.

"Not digital, Mr Lomas? I am surprised a man in your position is not more up to speed with the modern technology."

"I will get there one day but it is a good camera, I am happy with the results I can get from it."

"I notice that eleven shots have been taken."

"Yes, but none taken here though. It seemed to be inappropriate somehow. I thought to keep a few pictures as a lasting memento, but now I'm here I realise it is unnecessary." He spoke with an obvious sincerity that was beyond question. "In fact I have not taken one since I have been in Iraq. They are all from home I think. Auntie Margret's barbeque if I remember correctly."

Considering what the Iraqi held in his hands Lomas was surprised by how coolly he was reacting to his confrontational behaviour. The two vials hidden inside the camera could probably infect everyone and everything within a hundred miles radius of where they were now standing. He waited for the man in front of him to make the next move.

"How interesting," the officer replied, whilst showing very little interest at all. "But just to be on the safe side I must have the film. Would you mind removing it for me, Mr Lomas?"

He almost spat the words of the name. Their eyes never wavered from each other until with one hand the Arab tossed the camera back to Lomas, who caught it securely with two.

Lomas stripped out the film, closed the camera-back carefully and handed over the now worthless unwound roll of film to the smug security officer.

"There Mr Lomas. Now my president can rest more easily in his bed tonight in the knowledge that no anti-Iraqi propaganda will be turning up on the desk of British Military Intelligence, or the Director of the CIA. Dispose of this will you." The security man passed the ribbon of ruined film to the uniformed guard he had just reprimanded who jumped forward smartly to take it, although demure from his embarrassment.

"I doubt they would be interested in Auntie Margret's barbeque. Still she has one every year, I'll just have to take some more next summer. She's very old now though; she may not be around next summer. What a shame and I'll have no photographs to remind me of her and her wonderful barbeques."

"What a shame indeed. Now we can go? Mr Lomas, after you." Beneath his *shumagg* - the dark bearded face of the state security policeman may have been smiling as he ushered Lomas back onto the coach, but from beneath his *dishdashah* a protruding holstered pistol was testimony to his authority and seriousness.

Lomas complied and boarded the bus knowing he had only just got away with it. Khalid risked a glance towards Lomas as he passed him going towards his seat and thought, *shukran Allah. But if those vials aren't in his pockets where are they?* Khalid was sure though that the vials were now on the bus, and it was for that reason the drive home took twice as long as the outbound journey and was considerably smoother.

Chapter Four

Back to Baghdad

There was only silence among the passengers as the coach pulled out of the compound and headed north east into the coming evening. The westering sun on their left sent lengthening shadows across the desert turning every rock and tree into long, dark gashes in the sand. Much of the heat had gone from the day by this hour but still the air pulsing through the open windows felt hot on their faces. The two state security policemen sat together at the back talking quietly and quickly in Arabic to one another, their conversation rendered inaudible by the rhythmical din of the old diesel engine which propelled them towards Baghdad, a good meal and, maybe; a cold beer.

They sat apart from one another, the little group from the hotel; each to their own double seat. Fabien sat in the seat across the aisle from Lomas staring out at the moving shadow of the bus that stretched out across the desert floor to meet the oncoming darkness. Metzer was in the seat in front of him and was busy writing in his small notebook, and Mundai was dozing in the seat in front of Metzer. Lomas was considering what his next best course of action was going to be. It would be unlikely that anyone anytime soon would notice the two vials of Bessomthwaite 288 were missing; if ever. They were well hidden he thought and not a problem to get through Baghdad airport, but he had to get them out of Iraq as quickly as possible in case Khalid should have a sudden change of loyalty, but a sudden departure from Iraq of the newest member of the UN Weapons Inspection Team was bound to attract the attention of the security services, and restrict his movement when he needed to act quickly. He did not like ever to be in that position. He would also need to create a diversion and he would need a different passport. He was so engrossed in his plans, gazing off towards the setting sun across the hot and dusty barren waste that flashed by his window, he was startled when Fabien settled next to him and touched his arm.

"Pardonnez moi, monsieur, but what has happened 'ere?" She looked back over her shoulder to the where the two security policemen were sitting, not talking now but watching her as they bounced up and down with the rising and falling of the old coach on its ancient springs. "That man, he suspects you of something, Mr Lomas," she continued.

"Call me Eric, please. They only picked on me because I'm a Brit. We aren't terribly popular around here at the moment, as you no doubt appreciate," he assured her.

"And I am not a fool either, Eric," stated Günter Metzer, who had stuck his face between the two seat backs and was looking straight at him. Lomas resisted the temptation to punch it. "They checked your papers thoroughly enough didn't they, and yet didn't bother much with ours. Why? You are not in any trouble are you, Mr Lomas? Are we in danger now because of you?"

She began to cry. A soft wailing moan of a cry at first, then long quiet low sobs, full of all the other crying gone before; they sounded like the retchings of a grieving soul left with only this primal expression at the final realisation of total and absolute loss. This was pathos, this touched Lomas in a way that burrowed into him like a worm. It reminded him of his own pain, opened up the place within him where his loss lay, where his pain was hidden. He took her small hands in his. She looked up into his face and saw the sorrow that lay behind his cold blue eyes. She saw in that instant a connection between her grief and his and how it had turned to anger.

"Can you do something about what happened there?" she asked hopefully. "I am a nurse back home in France and I have a notion what killed them; by the description of the injuries and the time scale."

"I must," said Lomas. He noticed Mundai shifting in his seat, perhaps trying to listen in to their conversation. He raised a finger to his lips and Metzer took the hint immediately.

"So, where shall we eat tonight?" he asked. "Together, I hope."

"That would be nice," Fabien agreed, but Lomas seemed less than enthusiastic. "Oh, Eric, you must come too and protect me from the advances of this German," she whispered in his ear.

"I have to leave for home as soon as possible, tonight if there is a flight."

"I too fly to Paris tonight for home at midnight. Maybe there will be spare seats," Fabien begged. "Please dine with us, there is time.

"Well, there are no flights to Heathrow until tomorrow afternoon, and they have stopovers at Charles De Galle. Dinner sounds marvellous, and after I'll escort you to the airport and book a flight."

"Parfait." *That is a perfect outcome*, she thought. Having seen the pain he was still suffering she relished the chance to get to know this quiet, interesting man better.

"But not in the hotel, too many walls with ears I think," said Lomas. "And if I am not mistaken here comes one of those walls with ears now."

Mundai moved down the coach towards the group. His two colleagues from Directorate 5 were taking little to no interest at all in their surveillance targets. One picked his teeth while the other stared disinterestedly through the open window into the desert that their bus sped past as it rumbled ever nearer to Baghdad. At least they are not getting in my way, Mundai thought, wryly, whist still rather hoping they would be prepared to get in the way if any bullets started flying about.

"Ah, Herr Mundai." Günter picked up the thread Lomas had laid down. "We were thinking of eating before going back to the hotel, can you suggest anywhere decent in Baghdad?"

"There are many fine establishments in Baghdad that cater for the international palate," Mundai replied, a little annoyed by the inference Metzer had made. "Even under the strict imposition of the UN sanctions the wealthy of this world still expect to eat well. However, in the Medina, I know many restaurants where you will receive a warm welcome and wonderful food."

"Will you join us too, Mundai?" Fabien asked. Lomas and Metzer shot a glance towards one another, but it was done. They both had questions that could not be asked in Mundai's presence.

To their relief Mundai declined saying, "How kind of you, mademoiselle. Unfortunately, I have to rescue my three daughters from their auntie and get them to bed. They have school in the morning. I'll get Khalid to drop you at the Medina and I'll show you where to go that is very good."

The truth was Mundai and Khalid had to report to the general on their arrival in Baghdad after they had taken the bus back to the depot. So his daughters would have to stay the night with their aunt. She would be the one to get them ready for school in the morning. She was not going to be happy.

Khalid Nazim al Tikriti, his father, was an old friend of the general's and only a few years before had been his superior. He was a step brother of the President and had been feared and respected in equal measure in much the same way the general was now. But he and Saddam fell out over some minor internal security issue and he was subsequently stripped of all his power and position. He now lived with the very real threat of execution, and was only given unimportant missions to keep him in the fold but out of harm's way. With Saddam's sword of Damocles hanging over his head, these were operations no one else wanted but which he was unlikely to refuse. In the process Khalid had become an effective operative for General Mahmud Hassan's office, although this operation in particular had made Khalid suspicious of the general's motives. Even so, when Mundai asked him to drop Lomas and the other two off at the Medina and not at the hotel, Khalid felt that the general should be informed, so that back-up was in place to meet them when the coach arrived back in Baghdad, to maintain the surveillance. Mundai agreed and thanked his father for his wisdom.

The bleakness of the desert had given way to fruit orchards and almond groves and signs of habitation spread out from either side of the dusty road over which they rumbled. Metzer had returned to taking notes, Lomas now sat alone and Fabien had returned to her seat. She looked over towards him every so often, but he was looking out the window. He is quite good looking she thought. She took another look; and keeps fit. She looked down quickly at her clasped hands in case he suddenly looked over at her. He had strong hands but a gentle face. She had seen in him the pain he had been through. She wanted to kiss it better and help him resurrect himself from his misery. She found herself staring straight at him, and he was staring straight back at her. She could feel him staring into her and she became embarrassed and coy and quickly looked back down to her hands. Now he was sitting next to her. Now his strong but gentle hands held hers and she placed her head on his chest. Without speaking they sat holding one another's sadness together. They were both comfortable in their positions and eventually Fabien slept, Lomas feeling the shallow rise and fall of her head on his chest as she breathed. The thudding drum in him had become too insistent to ignore and he slipped slowly into caring how she might be when she woke, and who would look out for her when she returned to her home. Then he felt a pang of guilt when he remembered Katherine, but he had not felt like this with her. He found himself hoping Fabien would feel the same way about him, that she would want to take care of him.

You're going soft, man, he said to himself. And then he asked himself, so what if I am? For the first time in his adult life he felt good being alive, good being a warm blooded human being, not a killing machine. But the dusty old bus swept along taking him back to his past and to an unpredictable future. He wanted the world to stop so he could sit forever with her head on his chest and watch the gentle draught of her warm breath moving the dark hair on his forearm.

Soon it was night and the cooler evening wind blew in through the open window onto them and she woke. Lomas strectched up to pull the window shut and sat down again. When he did she moved her head and let it lightly rest on his shoulder.

"Hi," she said softly.

"Hello, sleepy."

"You are too comfortable. I hope you didn't mind?"

"Not at all. I find you comfortable too."

"Really?" She looked up at him, his face only centimetres away from hers.

"You looked so peaceful and untroubled." He wanted to kiss her full and open mouth, but it was neither the time nor the place.

She laid her head on his chest again, for a moment she had thought he was going to kiss her. As she drifted back into sleep Fabien admitted she wished he had.

Then suddenly they were in the city again and the bright lights of Baghdad. Moths and many other flying things, drawn by the street lights, buzzed them as the three of them stepped from the bus. Mundai gave them directions to a restaurant he knew they would enjoy.

"The owner is from my brother-in-law's family. She is a wonderful cook; her tagine is the most fragrant and tender goat I have ever tasted. You'll love it," he told them from the open door of the bus as it pulled away. He, Khalid and the old bus with its remaining passengers swept off in a cloud of dust into the Baghdad night, taking State Security with them. Lomas, Fabien and Günter Metzer were on their own then; three infidels, barbarians, in the heart of a simmering, hostile city.

Mundai had Khalid drop them at the gates of the ancient Medina. Beneath the palm trees, bathed in the orange light from the street lights, the chairs and tables that lined the walls of the ancient citadel were already beginning to fill up with small groups of men, young and old. The Baghdad men-folk, some in western clothes, others in the more traditional *dishdashah and shumagg,* were gathering as usual to sit and drink tea in the early evening and discuss the events of the day with their friends. Some were playing cards or chess while they chatted, or backgammon, some smoked scented tobaccos through tall thin bubbling water-pipes, and others were drinking mint tea brewed in ornate samovars that sent fragrant clouds of steam up into the evening air. But the UN's sanctions were really biting hard into Iraqi life and Saddam Hussein's propaganda machine had left the ordinary Iraqi in no doubt who was to blame. Each cabal of men in turn stopped and in silence watched the three Europeans approach and walk past before resuming their recreation. They paused, pawns poised in hands, hovering, over their chequered boards, their smoke stopped bubbling through the water-filled glass bowls of their *narghiles,* glasses of mint tea stopped halfway to lips. These sudden and spontaneous outbursts of inactivity, like an inverted Mexican wave, followed after them as they moved along the road and into the medina.

The thinly disguised undercurrent of hostility, which the three of them had inferred was not only dangerous but almost carnivorous, seemed to grow in its intensity as they pushed through the close narrow thoroughfares and alleyways of the medina until suddenly and without warning Lomas stopped, drawing Fabien and Metzer to him.

"We are being followed. Can we lose them?" he asked Metzer.

"Come with me. I know of a place where we will not be noticed and we can eat well too." With that Günter gripped Fabien's hand, turned quickly and disappeared into a crowded noisy bazaar without waiting for Lomas to follow.

Pushing through the great press of people that barred his way, Lomas struggled to keep up with the others. They twisted their way round rolls of carpets and rugs, were baulked by glinting mountains of intricately filigreed brass pots. They slipped in the wet blood from the halaal butchers, and were repulsed by the glazed eyed severed head and dripping lungs of a goat hanging there, covered in flies as testaments to the freshness of the meat sold there. They rushed, panting, past spice dealers and were shouted after by saffron sellers they had stepped over and ignored. Onward they pressed through the stench of blood and death, and sweat and dust.

At last they passed through a small low door in a flaking, crumbling wall and found themselves in a high walled narrow alleyway filled with the fetor of coffee and urine, faeces and jasmine. An old mangy dog slunk amongst the rubbish of rotting commerce, each rib and moving bone well defined by his hunger as he trotted by them. A beggar woman half-blind with disease clung to a scrawny baby that bawled and bawled from malnutrition. The woman pulled at their clothes gently, hand up as they passed, implying please give something.

They stopped and pulled some dinar from their pockets. Lomas collected the few coins and handed them to the wretch.

"Shukran sayid, saafar fee ri'aayat Allah." (Thank you, sir, travel in the protection of God) murmured the old crone.

Thank you, thought Lomas. I need any help I can get.

"Where are we?" asked Fabien.

"End of this alleyway at the top of the hill is the main concourse. More for tourists than for locals though, but at least the air will be a little fresher." Günter knew Baghdad well and was keen to get somewhere less putrid than their present location.

"We'll have lost our escorts I suspect," said Lomas when they began walking again.

"Yes, but why did we have to run? We have done nothing wrong," insisted Fabien.

"No," Günter replied, "but maybe there is someone here who has, on our behalf, eh Eric old boy?"

"I get paranoid sometimes. They were pick-pockets probably, scoping tourists" said Lomas.

"Pick-pockets indeed, I think our Mr Lomas is not at all what he seems, Fabien. I want some answers Buddy Boy." Metzer's exaggerated German American accent made Lomas smile despite his growing irritation with the man.

"Yes, I suppose you must both require some answers," Lomas conceded. "But you need the right questions first to get the answers you are looking for. Let us save the questions for the dinner table, when we are more relaxed."

They had reached the main concourse and there seemed to be a tacit agreement in their silence. They found somewhere to dine that looked clean and offering something resembling the local cuisine. Fabien went to the powder room to freshen up and the two men seated themselves at a table far enough away from the windows not to be easily seen from outside. The restaurant was crowded with early evening diners. Sanctions or no sanctions, the wealthy, as Mundai had suggested, were indeed always able to eat well, wherever they were.

"I can get you out," Günter whispered. He leant across the table to deliver his point more effectively. "I can get you out but, I need to know what it is you hide and why you run."

"Why do you think I am going anywhere?"

"The tail we had on the bus all day, and here as soon as we left the damned bus. They were no pick-pockets, were they?"

"And you Herr Metzer, I am guessing, are no reporter either."

"It is one of several hats you could say."

"Made in Langley perhaps?" Eric asked.

"No, actually, but you could say we are related, Eric." Metzer wanted to keep his cards close to his chest but could not resist showing off a bit. Lomas had a reputation that extended far beyond the borders of Britain. "My involvement is less dramatic, less conspicuous than yours is for your people. That is how I know it is you they are watching. They have never bothered with me before, and I have been here since before Kuwait. And Fabien, well she is no more than a bystander, wouldn't you agree?"

"Hardly a bystander, there is the small matter of the untimely death of her brother," said Lomas.

"Not enough for her to register on their radar though."

"No, I suppose not," Lomas agreed. "Okay, so what assistance do you think I need, and what will be your price for this assistance?" Lomas met Metzer's animated countenance with expressionless calm. His eyes gave nothing away of the intent behind them.

Günter Metzer was a neat methodical man. His well tailored suit hung well on him and, although dusty from the day, the light sandy coloured material still looked sharp and remarkably uncrumpled. He had a mop of fair hair but not blond. He was plump but not fat. His white shirt fitted him well enough at the collar to allow him to wear a tie throughout the day. He wore rough brushed leather desert boots, dirty and scuffed now but they were obviously expensive and well made. He would have been considered quite handsome were it not for a lazy eye. His left eyelid which never fully opened, nor seemingly ever fully closed, gave him the appearance of someone profoundly drunk yet, ironically, he seldom drank alcohol. This facial defect conspired against his sharpness of mind to confer on him a mildly simple minded expression which often led to others underestimating his prodigious intellectual abilities.

Eric Lomas was not one who fell into this category and had in that instant, determined the career of the inquisitive journalist should be terminated very soon. He liked to keep things tidy.

"Price? You insult me," Metzer complained. "We are on the same side after all, aren't we? I am a reporter, Mr Lomas, my currency is information. I can smuggle you out, with new papers and passport, but I need something I can send back to my people. I think you found something out there in the desert, and what is more they know you found something and are following you to see what you are going to do with it," said Metzer, continuing to speculate.

"I didn't find anything there. I was shown where it was." Lomas had already decided on Metzer's fate so telling him a little would only serve to leave him feeling unthreatened. "They know, as you seem to, what I do for a living and yet I have been led straight to a most sensitive and potentially dangerous discovery, why?"

"WMDs, I suspected so all along," said Metzer. "There was too much misinformation concerning what happened at Karbala for it to be anything else. What is it? Stockpiles of chemical weapons?"

"I can't tell you what it is. I haven't decided how to play this one out. Consider this over dinner if you will, but not a word to Fabien, understand?" Metzer nodded his agreement. Lomas continued, "Consider the idea that Saddam himself knows nothing about this, and that someone in the Mukhabarat is taking a tremendous gamble by setting me up. How does the picture look to you now?"

Metzer pondered a moment before replying. He weighed the possibilities against the probabilities. He sifted through the painstakingly researched background information he had gathered on Lomas and his previous operations. He was more than aware of the delicate balance of trust and suspicion that existed between Washington and London, and the fragile half-peace trembling here in Baghdad. He tried to assimilate all these separate elements to come up with one feasible theory to adequately illustrate the current position Lomas was in. This would enable him to provide Lomas with a perceptive solution to his dilemma.

"You imply a conspiracy within Party Intelligence," Metzer stated.

"Quite possibly, but not a conspiracy against the Party, nor the president necessarily," Lomas conceded. "I know the importance of what I have found and I am assuming they do too, and yet they are quite prepared to let me run with it in the hope it may work to Iraq's advantage. But I have my own issues to confront and my own agenda to work through. I have found hard physical evidence of what caused the appalling loss of life around Karbala, and what it was wiped out my entire family. No matter what, I have every intention of ensuring it can never happen again."

Günter Metzer leaned back on his chair and let the air whistle through his teeth. Already the cogs of his agile journalistic mind were turning on a story. "This could precipitate a second Gulf War."

"Indeed," agreed Lomas. "Now leave it alone until after dinner. Here she comes, not a word."

"Yeh, sure." Metzer pulled his notebook and a pen from a pocket inside his jacket and began to write, little suspecting he had already written his own death warrant.

Fabien joined them at the table and apologised for taking so long but she looked radiant again and had regained some of her natural composure and grace. Lomas stood as she approached and helped her with her chair. She smiled up at him as she sat down.

"Merci. Tu es très gentil," she purred.

Chapter Five

A Death for Dessert

"No more world affairs this evening I beg you both, the day has been too harsh, let's try to enjoy the evening. La soirée est pour le plaisir, n'est ce pas?"

The men agreed. Well done Fabien, thought Lomas. The evening, any evening, should be reserved for the pursuit of pleasure.

Günter continued with his jottings and Lomas summoned the waiter. He ordered a bottle of white wine imported from South Africa, for which Fabien nodded approval. Then they fussed over the menu together, laughing now and then. Günter was still writing in his journal unaware of their growing familiarity when he suddenly set down his pen and called over the waiter.

"My friends are unused to Iraqi food. Can you suggest some local dishes they might find to their taste?" Günter asked.

"Of course, sir," replied the waiter.

"Good idea, Metzer," Lomas conceded.

The waiter thought for a moment then proceeded to explain their forthcoming meal.

A *mezza* with *arak*, an aniseed flavoured aperitif, was suggested to start them off. Plates of small kebabs, spiced goat, beef and chicken on skewers with a side dish of *turshi,* which he explained is pickled mixed vegetables and yoghurt with pita breads, would be brought to their table. The rest he assured them would be an enjoyable surprise.

They ordered more wine, light red from Bordeaux this time, to complement the meats. They talked and ate quietly with Günter about Fabien's dead brother and her life in France.

"After Papa died, Mother slowly sank into alcoholism and became nothing more than a helpless drunk. It was tragic and so sad to watch. Her changes of mood eventually became so extreme and violent that she presented a danger to herself and others around her. Francoise arranged and paid for her to stay in an asylum until she improved, but she missed my father so much she only continued to deteriorate and she passed away two years ago. So now I am quite alone." She paused. "He was a wonderful brother, and my truest friend. He took care of me when I was young and we were both at school. He stepped in and took the place of the parents I still needed. He was eight years older than me and that makes a big difference when you are only nine. He took care of me. He became my hero. I miss him more than anyone. I loved him very much, but now, like all the others I have loved, he is gone."

The soup arrived, red lentil soup made with cumin and celery. The wine, and the small amount of amphetamine administered while in the powder-room, had put Fabien in a more self-confident, more relaxed mood. So although hers was a truly sad story, she seemed able to tell it with surprisingly little emotion, as if almost she had told the story many times and could tell it in this fashion without causing herself uncontrolled distress.

"He was thirty-three when he was killed, a year younger than I am now. It doesn't seem fair, all that talent lost; gone forever."

"Life is seldom fair, Fabien, least of all in war," said Günter, in an uncharacteristic display of empathy. "Life my dear becomes arbitrary when 'men let slip the dogs of war and chaos reigns when Ate strides unchallenged through the heads of men'. "

A German quoting Shakespeare, although paraphrasing, was an unexpected development.

"But you must already know this, being a nurse," he continued. "Life itself is the ultimate tragedy, and in war men are merely juggling with the power of death over life."

"But he was not at war with anyone. He was just out here doing his job. I suppose you could say he was unlucky, but then they all were, weren't they, the victims? Just incredibly unlucky, being in the wrong place at the wrong time," she said with resignation.

Beef with fruit and rice was next, and the flavours of apricots and apples and cinnamon were perfect with the highly spiced meat.

"Do you have other family, a husband perhaps, children?" Lomas asked her.

"No, no children and my ex-husband, I have not seen him for five years, since the divorce. He is working in a nightclub in Ayia Napa now, in sales he told me. Selling what, I can only imagine. Following Francoise's death I inherited everything; he had no family other than me. It has left me very comfortably off. And I have my work of course, but Jean-Piere could not live with the idea of being a kept man, so he left. I sold everything except our Paris apartment, and bought a cottage in a small village near the sea and now I spend as much of my free time as I can there. I stay at the apartment in Madeleine when I am working of course. Clinique Matignon is only three stops on the Metro from Madeleine, two if I walk to La

Concorde. In the summer I prefer to walk all the way. I can be at the hospital in around fifteen, twenty minutes. It is such a lovely walk, round Église de la Madeleine and down Rue Royale to Place de la Concorde and then along Avenue Gabriel. It is as if I am walking in woodland, the trees are so close to each other. I think it is the most beautiful part of Paris. I walk right past the gardens of the President's palace and then I am there, on Avenue Matignon. But even though it is a very pleasant apartment, and it has a balcony that overlooks the walnut trees that line the street below and there are plenty of good shops and restaurants near by, Paris is just so busy with tourists in the summer that I long to be in the country." She had returned there now in her mind and was smiling at the thought of it. "That is where I am going to be tomorrow."

"Where in the country is your home?" Lomas asked.

"It's not really in the country I suppose. It is a fishing village near the sea on the estuary of the river Rance, near St Malo. A place called Saint Luc de Vilaine in the department of Ille-et-Vilaine, in Brittany. It is about four hours drive from Paris, but I seldom drive these days. I have a little car at the cottage but I rarely use it for long trips. The flight from Charles de Gaulle to Rennes is about an hour. And then it is an hour's drive home."

Flat bread with fruit jelly followed and then coffee; strong and pungent, creamed and sweetened. Even Metzer had to admit it was the best coffee he had ever tasted.

"They are very particular about their coffee here; in Iraq generally I mean. After it is ground they heat it and cool it, nine times to remove any impurities. It is this treatment that gives this coffee its unique flavour." Metzer knew his subject. "Did you both enjoy the meal?"

Lomas and Fabien both agreed they had.

"I am so pleased I was able to contribute to the evening. I was beginning to feel a little like a spare wheel."

"Nonsense you have both been perfect gentlemen, but I have eaten far too much. It was all too delicious for me to stop myself," Fabien admitted.

"I too," said Lomas, "but I understand this is considered to be somewhat of a compliment to the chef, in these parts."

"Are you about to belch then, Eric?" Fabien asked, and they all laughed.

"I sincerely hope not, but afraid the small amount of wine I drank has left me with an urgent need for the lavatory. Will you both excuse me I have to go to the little boy's room?"

"Me too," said Günter, English grammar failing him momentarily in his excitement. He did not want Lomas out of his sight. He was pretty sure Eric carried something of great importance and he wanted to be in on the deal at the start. They stood beside one another as they relieved themselves. The urinal was cramped with hardly enough space for two men and their elbows touched. Lomas had finished and was zipping his fly but Metzer still needed to complete the job in hand. So in order to keep Lomas a little longer he ventured, "Now Eric, about your dilemma."

Günter looked up into the cold eyes of his companion as he spoke and immediately recognised the intent within them. He was zipping his fly as he tried in vain to quickly raise his left hand to defend himself but it was too late. The clenched hand with which Lomas hit him felt as if it had passed through him. It did stop his heart though and now was pinning him against the opposite wall. He was aware of being dragged into an alleyway, the smell of pungent smoke rising from a large pile of rubbish and small yellow and crimson flames licking at his right ear. He felt his head being grabbed violently from behind, which produced enough impetus to snap his neck and spinal cord like a breadstick. Suddenly there was no light, no flickering from the fire in which he now laid, motionless. Then all the pain had gone. He felt nothing and then; there was nothing.

Lomas stooped over Günter's lifeless body and removed the wallet and passport from his suit jacket. He threw out the travel passes onto the fire beside the body and pocketed the passport. There were Diners Club and American Express cards in the name of Metzer and something like two thousand dinars in one hundred and two hundred and fifty dinars notes, but these were not what he was searching for. Then, tucked inside the lining of the wallet, Lomas found the CIA identity card he knew had to be there somewhere. The card did not refer anywhere to the CIA. It showed a small picture of Metzer and the name Peter Hansen above a bar code strip. A small square micro-chip in the top left hand corner of the card would have given Metzer direct access to the main-frame computer at CIA headquarters in Langley, Virginia; from anywhere in the world where he could get a decent satellite link. Lomas removed it from behind the lining and threw the wallet with its remaining contents into the flames. Metzer lay face down in the very heart of the fire. His hair and the shoulders and arms of his jacket, had begun to blacken and char, and had now broken out into small plumes of orange flame.

Lomas covered the partially incinerated body with some pieces of old carpet and wooden boxes he found nearby. Soon enough the police would not be able to identify this corpse so easily, and that would give him some time, some breathing space to work out just what he was going to do with the contents of his innocuous looking camera. That it held within it the fate of some many unknowing and unknown victims was still Lomas's secret. Lomas looked at the face in the small picture on the identity card he held in his hand. He re-read the name Peter Hansen, but the face was still Günter's face. However, now if the police eventually identified the incinerated body as Günter Metzer's, the *Mukhabarat* (Iraqi Intelligence) could not establish that he was in fact Peter Hansen – CIA agent and that would make Lomas's own escape from Iraq that much easier. But more importantly, Lomas thought as he tossed the small notebook into the heart of the flames, Günter Metzer's suppositions regarding Lomas's find in the desert were incinerating with him, and not forming the main feature in a report on a desk in Langley.

He could perhaps make use of this other passport too, but later for that he thought. Back to Fabien and a short stay in France; perhaps.

When he returned to the table he gave Fabien an apology on Günter's behalf.

"He had a call from his office. A possible story that needed looking into."

"I may not see him again then?" she asked.

"I would say that's unlikely, if you are leaving tonight." He considered quickly how he would ask her to assist him.

"Nor will I see you again after tomorrow, after this evening even, if there are no seats available on tonight's flight," she said sadly.

"Does that bother you then?" he asked.

"Of course. Do you not know we have connected?"

"Yes, I know. Well, I had hoped." That drum began beating again. She laid her hand on his softly and pulled at his middle finger. Those drums, those almost forgotten drums were now pounding in his ears. "I have to pack up my bag at the hotel, but I can come with you to the airport and try for a seat on your flight if you would allow me to accompany you to Paris, at least," he suggested.

"You are a true gentleman indeed. Yes, I would appreciate that very much," she admitted. "Then perhaps I'll have time to persuade you to come see my cottage in Saint Luc, sometime, maybe."

"We shall see," said Lomas. *Parfait*, thought Lomas: perfect.

Chapter Six

Flight from Baghdad

Fabien paid her bill at the hotel's reception and thanked the young Arab for her comfortable stay. The young man blushed a little and told her she would be welcome any time she chose to return. She had changed into clean white linen slacks and a plain red tee shirt which seemed to encourage her body alone to give it form. Her brown feet, barely covered by a pair of open silver sling back shoes, displayed the painted nails of her toes in the same blood red as her torso. She wore very little make-up, as was her habit. So simple, so classy. The boy at reception thought she looked lovely, even in her travelling clothes.

Fabien wandered over to and sat in a large leather chair near the hotel foyer's grand entrance with her luggage and watched as some of the other guests left in taxis to go out for the evening, to dine or dance into the early hours. It was nearly ten now and she began to wonder if Eric had changed his mind. A waiter came up to her.

"Would madam like something to drink, perhaps a glass of mint tea?" he asked.

"You are kind, but no thank you. I am waiting for a friend who is taking me to the airport."

The waiter bowed and wished her bon voyage. Eric appeared from the lift, waved to her and he walked across to reception to pay his bill at the desk before joining her in the foyer.

"Taxi is on its way," he told her. He preferred to remain standing but she remained poised and sitting. "Is this all your luggage?" he asked, noticing she had just the one case and a hand-bag with a red sweater hung over it.

"Yes. I did not intend to stay any longer than necessary. But I appear not to travel as lightly as you."

They both looked down at the brown leather valise he was holding. "Just a couple of shirts and fresh swimming trunks, what more does one need?" he said.

"A shower perhaps. What have you been doing all this time?" She had noticed that he had put on a fresh shirt, but he had not shaved and although his jacket was clean and smart, his trousers and shoes were those he had worn in the desert that afternoon.

"I telephoned the airport to find a seat on your flight. There was one left in first class, so you'll have to bribe the steward to let you come and see me."

"I am in first class too, but I am not sure I would wish to see you at all. You haven't even bothered to shave, and you stink." She caressed his shin with the painted nails of her left foot and smiled. "But that may not be at all bad," she added.

"I can shave and freshen up on the plane. It is first class you know."

"You have no need to bother on my account; I had forgotten what Man smells like."

"Why Madame, I do believe you are shameless."

"Let's wait and see shall we."

In truth Lomas had spent most of the time whilst Fabien was packing, in his room replacing Metzer's passport photograph with one of his own. Using a thin bladed knife he kept on his key-ring and hot water, Lomas had managed to separate the laminate sheet from the paper beneath. Over

Günter's mug shot he slipped a photograph of himself, which he had removed from the travel documents Mundai had given him earlier that day. Sealing the laminate back in place again had been difficult and had to be just right, so the document would look unchanged. He remembered a trick shown to him by one of the bio-chemists working with his mother, when he was a boy. By mixing two readily available personal hygiene products and a little saliva, a highly effective and most importantly, transparent, adhesive could be made to stick his mediocre school report back together. This he found gave the effect he required and even after close scrutiny, this new passport, he was forced to conclude, was a masterpiece. No one would spot the change: except perhaps under x-ray. He would just have to take that chance. He opened and closed the passport two or three times more before he was totally satisfied and had finally convinced himself he could use it instead of his own.

The taxi arrived and a bell boy was on hand immediately to lift Fabien's small case into the boot. Lomas tipped the boy but kept his bag with him in the cab. As the taxi pulled away for the airport a door opened behind the reception desk of the hotel. Mundai slipped out and spoke to the young Arab boy.

"Did either of them ask to say good-bye to Herr Metzer?" he asked.

"Yes, sir, the lady asked if he was in the hotel, but Herr Metzer still has not returned. You see his key is still in its box," the boy replied, pointing to a box in the vast rack of numbered pigeon holes behind him.

"Interesting. What did Mr Lomas say?"

"Nothing about Herr Metzer, sir."

"Okay, fine. Thank you. You have done well."

"Shukran lak sayid," the boy thanked him back.

On the way to the airport Fabien mentioned that she had tried to call Metzer's room but that he had been out still.

"I'd have liked at least to say good-bye," she said.

"I think the heat got to him today," said Lomas with no sense of remorse whatsoever. It was already gone midnight and Lomas was tired and getting anxious to board a plane, any plane out of Iraq. If he could successfully avoided detection by airport security, he would be able then to put his feet up and relax a bit.

Although security had been stepped up in airports across the world generally after the Lockerbie bombing in 1988, it is easy to forget how much easier it was to pass through an airport at the beginning of the new millennium. Before the attacks in New York on September 11, security at most major airports was at best perfunctory. The bag Lomas carried with him at all times passed through security without a hitch and the work he had done to Metzer's passport proved to be virtually foolproof. However, Fabien saw Lomas produce a German passport when he was required to show his before boarding. She was no fool and although she considered this to be a little odd, decided to make no mention of it there and then at passport control. Fortunately she never did make the connection between Eric's German passport and Metzer's sudden disappearance. If she had, events could very well have turned out much differently.

She had removed from her suitcase an expensive cashmere jacket before boarding the aircraft, which the steward took from her straight away and placed on a hanger for her somewhere during the flight. She knew, from previous experience, it would be at least ten degrees cooler when they arrived in Paris, than it was in Baghdad. Another steward escorted her to the first class lounge and the large booth in which she could enjoy her personal space. La Premier Class, Air France, is all about personal space and unadulterated luxury. From the champagne to the merino wool blanket for the full length bed and from the personal closet space to the comfortable bench for your guests to come sit with you in your personal space, it was out of this world and a complete contrast to the deprivation and abject poverty they were leaving behind.

Lomas followed on behind carrying his own bag, much to the chagrin of his insistent attendant. The flight to Paris was scheduled to leave at two a.m. but, after a slight delay for a couple of late arrivals, they took off at twenty past the hour. The flight was to be about eight hours' duration, long enough for them both to get some sleep in the sumptuous beds their seats folded into if required, and meant they would arrive at Charles de Galle just in time for breakfast there. They were across the aisle from one another, with no one in between and the rest of first class seemed unoccupied. Lomas ordered champagne for them both and went to the bathroom to shave and generally refresh himself.

"Caviar? What a wonderful idea," Lomas remarked when he returned. "There are a couple of businessmen further down but they are snoring already. Tonight it is just us. I wonder would the pretty lady like to join me for a little light supper and a nightcap."

"The caviar is complimentary, as is the champagne," replied Fabien. She came over and sat across the table from him on the comfortable bench seat provided for such occasions. "First Class really means first class with Air France. I am proud to be French, as you can see."

"Nothing wrong with that, this is very civilized indeed," he said looking around his personal space. "I wish I could say I was as proud to be English at this moment."

He poured the champagne in silence. He handed Fabien a filled glass and passed to her the croutons of caviar. She bit into one and savoured the salty fish eggs that popped between her teeth, and sipped her champagne, letting the bubbles dance across her tongue, with an elegance that suggested to Lomas she was not unfamiliar with this level of luxury. He took a long pull from his glass before continuing.

"We talk a good game us English, and we are good people. We have always stood up against dictators and championed the oppressed, but there is always some little shit from somewhere high up in our governmental system, who dreams up a scheme to boost his personal cache and private wealth. These squalid little men do all us good Englishmen a great disservice by degrading the way we view ourselves and it's this which eventually tarnishes the image others have of us abroad. These small acts of corruption end up dragging us all down to a level of immorality where, no matter how honourable we may have felt before to be English, we are left feeling cheap and abused, like a tired old prostitute on a cold and lonely morning."

"Wow! Another glass of champagne, Mr Churchill? What a speech." Fabien was enthralled by his passion. He had always seemed so calm and in control.

"I am so sorry. What must you think?" he replied.

"I think it is encouraging that you feel you can confide to me things like this. No need to apologise for that," she said. "I know nothing about you really, do I?"

"It might be best you don't." He did not want her to become a loose end that he would need to deal with, certainly not in the fashion he had needed to deal with Herr Metzer. He had grown to like her in the short space of time he had been in her company, and if anything he was beginning to feel a strong desire to make sure no further harm came to her. "If I told you I would have to kill you," he joked.

"You *are* a spy. I thought so. That's why you travel on a German passport."

"You noticed." Lomas said sadly. Perhaps he would have to kill her after all.

"Of course I noticed. I am not just some dumb blonde you picked up in an Ayia Napa night club."

He noted the reference to her ex-husband, and saw her loneliness returning.

"Indeed you are not."

"Did Günter get the passport for you?"

"In a manner of speaking, he did yes. Now he was a spy, did you guess that?"

"No! Really? How do you know he is?" she asked, leaving Eric's unintended error of tense unnoticed.

"CIA. That's why he latched on to me," replied Lomas evading her direct questioning.

"So what is it you do then exactly? I doubt you are a full time weapons inspector," Fabien challenged.

"I am just a civil servant. I deal with military and security problems for the Crown of England. I am more of a fixer than an agent provocateur, but I have been non-operational for six months now, since the names of those who died at Karbala were announced. They felt I might be too unstable once I knew for certain my wife and boys were dead. They would only allow me to come here once I had agreed to travel incognito as a UN weapons inspector. As you saw today that did not work." Lomas lowered his head and stare into his empty glass.

Fabien got up and filled his glass with the remainder of the wine and sat on his knee. Her hands went through his hair gently and then she kissed him softly on his forehead.

"Let me help you. Let me try to repair you. I am an experienced psychiatric nurse, and I have the cottage in Brittany where you are welcome to stay for as long as you wish, or as long as it takes to put you back together again."

"Keep talking, I might just take you up on that offer," he warned her.

"I mean it; come. I have a month or so compassionate leave remaining before I have to think about going back to Paris. Come now, the sun lives in my house by the river," she said, trying to encourage him to agree.

It was lyrical, like something his late wife Katherine would have said. He could feel himself becoming drawn to this fascinating woman, and Lomas began to wonder whether his mission would suffer if he allowed himself the indulgence of spending a few more days in her company. If nothing else it would give him time to think how he was to proceed once he was back in England. Better yet, he stood a better chance of entering the country undetected by using a south coast port such as Plymouth. There would be a much higher risk of him being stopped at Heathrow or Dover, than at Poole or Weymouth. If he could get to St Helier on Jersey or St Peter Port on Guernsey, from there he would be nothing more than a day tripper, a tourist.

"Let's sleep on it," he advised. Fabien agreed sleep was required, so she pushed the button to summon a steward. A steward arrived and removed the tray of glasses and plates from Eric's table after showing them how easily each of their chairs converted into a comfortable bed. The steward said he would call on them half an hour before landing so they could both freshen themselves for their onward journey.

Chapter Seven

Mundai's Morning

Baghdad never really sleeps, it just slows down a little between two and five o'clock in the morning. Even in this quieter hollow of the night people still continue to go about their business and to enjoy themselves, taking full advantage of the cooler night air. Everything seems just a tiny bit calmer and less frantic through those few hours. But in the quieter district of the city, despite being exhausted, Mundai nervously paced up and down the tiny office behind reception in a mild panic.

It had been a long day and even though he knew making *Salah* was not obligatory for persons on a long journey Mundai felt strained and agitated. He had only made valid *Salah* once, the *fajr*, first thing in the day. He knew any Muslims who did not pray five times a day were considered sinners at the very least. He was afraid he would become a sinner himself or worse, that he would be denounced as a disbeliever for not observing each *Adhan* called throughout the day.

He had heard the muezzins calling him to prayer but each time he knew he would have been unable to give the time to perform valid *Salah*. So he had tried to use a small room at the Bahr al-Mihl visitors' centre which had been reserved for just that purpose to perform *dhuhr* and *asr* together, which was permissible. But his mind had been full of worry for the successful outcome of his mission.

He missed *maghrib* completely so he had laid out his mat in the office, having finally returned to the hotel late in the evening, and performed *maghrib* and *isha* combined, but his heart still wasn't really in it.

He worried that he was becoming a bad Muslim, a Godless person. In the daily routine of *Adhan* and *Salah* there was a pattern to his life which kept him centred and helped him achieve an inner calmness that carried him through the rest of each day, but it was gone one thirty now and he was feeling harried.

Although he had managed to grab some food from the kitchen on his return, Mundai felt tired and hungry and he needed his bed. He had already waited as long as he dared for Metzer to return. He hadn't arrived back with the other two and his key was still on its peg in reception.

Was it possible that even now Metzer could emerge as an important player in this whole conspiracy? Mundai wondered.

He had never spoken to anyone about his suspicions regarding Herr Metzer, but as he left the hotel to take the short cab ride across town to see the general, he wondered if he should have mentioned his misgivings regarding Metzer before. Given that he had no real evidence to support these doubts Mundai concluded it was probably better he kept his suspicions to himself.

And then there was the thought of Nadia, his mean spirited sister-in-law, giving him the jitters. He knew she had not understood his predicament. She had always thought Mundai's children should come first, before his job at the hotel. But she could have no idea how important his work there really was, so he had never been able to tell her. The general had to be advised of this latest and unexpected development no matter what time of the day or night and she would have to accept that and he had told her so.

Now, sitting in the back seat of the taxi, he regretted speaking to her so harshly. She was a kindly soul really, and it was not his usual way of speaking to women. He often wished he could be more like other men who stood up to their womenfolk and treated them as nothing more than chattels. But he had loved his late wife without compromise and throughout their marriage he had done anything she asked of him to save her from unhappiness. It was his habit now and he preferred to treat all women in this way, even his wife's unpleasant sister, so it vexed him that he had spoken to her in such an unpleasant fashion. He wished he could worry less about everything and remain cool and confident no matter what was thrown at him; like his father. Why couldn't he be more like him, a man who allowed life to merely wash over him?

Tonight, however, even Khalid had the jitters. He was already waiting in the general's outer office when Mundai arrived. He had bathed and he was clean shaven apart from the neatly trimmed grey walrus moustache he always kept. He had changed his dusty desert clothes for clean western style trousers and freshly pressed shirt open at the collar. On his feet he wore new white canvas shoes and he had in his best set of sparking white teeth. It was hard to believe it was the same man who had driven the bus earlier that day. He looked sharp.

They sat two chairs apart in a small room with no window somewhere in the *Mukhabarat* building, both nervously watching the minutes tick by. They did not speak to each other at first, just nodded.

"Still no sign of him?" Khalid asked, eventually. Mundai shook his head.

"Did you perform *Salah* yesterday?" he asked.

"No, but one day off won't hurt." Khalid was not fussed about following the muezzin's instruction but he did read the Qur'an regularly. "You?" he asked.

"Only once, first thing," Mundai complained. "I tried again later, twice, but I don't think they will count for anything."

"You'll burn in the fires of Satan, boy." He laughed but Mundai remained unimpressed.

"You going out after this then?" he asked, noticing for the first time his father's dramatic change in appearance.

"Yes. I thought I'd like to get drunk at my club on Scotch whisky while I am waiting for the American armies to arrive." He spoke in an exaggeratedly posh English accent. They both laughed away some of their anxiety and fell silent again.

On the wall above the general's closed door the clock showed ten to two. Facing them the general's aide sat writing at a table. When the intercom on his table buzzed the aide picked up the telephone receiver and just listened for a moment, then replaced the hand set in its cradle.

"You may go in now. The general wishes to see you both together." The aide stood and opened the door for them and closed it quietly behind them again after ushering them inside.

"It has gone well today, you think?" asked General Mahmud. "Please sit both of you."

"I'd say so," replied Mundai when they had sat down. "But would it not have been easier to just arrest this man and then simply show the UN inspection team the weapons they are looking for?" he asked.

"My head would very soon after be found on a spike above the gates of the Presidential Palace, together with the heads of all those associated with me," the general assured them. He turned to Khalid. "You know that."

Khalid nodded his agreement.

"Besides," continued the general, "in doing that we catch only the one fish. So what is there to lose? My way we lose one big fish but maybe catch a net full."

"And you, Khalid, my dear friend, what is your assessment of today's efforts, successful?"

"He has those two vials and has left the hotel with the girl, Mundai tells me. I guess by now he is on a plane bound for Paris. So, all we have to do now is wait for the news reports of a mysterious pandemic to hit London and your plan of great retribution has been a complete success. Yes, I think it has gone well today," Khalid summarised.

"Not quite. Yes, all that you say would be true but for the fact that Lomas did not get on the plane with the girl, a German journalist named Metzer did." The general spoke softly to them but it was plain he could barely contain his annoyance.

"What?" Khalid exclaimed. The seriousness of the situation was clear to Khalid. A foreign agent loose in the city with pockets full of anthrax bacillus 288 was less than ideal.

"That's impossible," Mundai blurted out. "With respect sir, I saw Lomas and the girl come back to the hotel at nine thirty. Herr Metzer was not with them. At midnight, they both paid their bills and left for the airport together in a taxi. I heard Lomas ask for the airport. Metzer has not returned to the hotel at all this evening."

"He must have gone earlier to the airport to book the flight and met her there. If Lomas was only taking her to the airport then, where is Lomas now he is not on that plane?" Khalid's voice began to sound uncharacteristically panicked. "What if he should decide to seek revenge on us rather than his own people? I have seen what that sort of stuff did to the Iranians during the war. There is no escaping it."

"He must be found and neutralised as safely as possible before he has a chance to release this deadly Bessomthwaite 288 micro-organism here in Baghdad." The general was calm but understandably worried. He had known there was always a risk this could happen. "If we can't clear this up quickly enough ourselves, all sections of *Mukhabarat* will have to be mobilised. This means I will have to relinquish operational control to Directorate Nine and probably face some very awkward questions from members of Directorate Six, which I was hoping to avoid until much later. Have no fear brothers I shall ensure neither of you are implicated in this. Should heads need to roll it will be mine alone."

"With respect, General, I can't see Metzer leaving the hotel without paying his bill," Mundai interrupted. "His work is here. He virtually lives here now. I think he would be unlikely to jeopardise that. Again, with respect, sir, let's not be too hasty." Mundai could feel the eyes and the total attention of the other two bearing down on him, and he enjoyed the rare moment. They were both taking him seriously for once, so he decided to continue.

"I have often wondered recently whether Herr Metzer is not in fact something other than the annoying little journalist he has made us all believe he is. The CIA would have reason enough to assist Lomas, if my supposition is correct. Phone the airport again and ask the immigration officer to describe the man who accompanied the nurse. Passports can be forged can they not? So long as the face holding the passport matches the face in the passport, height and age assessment demands more than just a cursory glance at a document. And you did, if I remember, General, instruct them at the airport to leave her companion unhindered."

"Indeed I did, Mundai, indeed I did," said the general picking up the telephone receiver. He issued a series of brusque instructions to his aide and the three waited in silence.

With the receiver still in his hand the general suddenly spoke into it again. "It was definitely Metzer's passport? You are sure? Do you remember the man? Hold on then. Mundai, come here and talk to this person who could very soon be out of a job."

The general held out the receiver to Mundai. Mundai took it warily from the general's outstretched hand and spoke into it.

"Yes, hello, the man you say is Günter Metzer. Did he have a lazy eye?" There was a pause. "One eye half closed, the other normal." Mundai placed a hand over the mouthpiece. "Where do they find these people General?" he asked in frustration. The general threw his hands up in the air and stared up at the ceiling, smiling.

"Well, how tall was he?" Mundai continued, talking to the immigration officer on the other end of the phone line again. "What do you mean, average for a European? No that's not short, you're right. His eyes, yes, go on, what was special about his eyes? Piercing, piercing blue, like in his photograph. No, that's fine. Yes, thanks for your help. Keep up the good work." Mundai put down the receiver. "It wasn't Metzer that got on the plane with the nurse, it was definitely Lomas."

The general sat back down, behind his desk and breathed a sigh of relief. He thought how close they might have come to disaster, although if he had known at the time Günter Metzer's true whereabouts he need never have worried.

Mundai sat back down next to Khalid who asked, "How can you be so sure it was Lomas?"

"We can go and scan through the closed circuit TV discs later to be certain if you wish, General, but that was Lomas with the nurse not Metzer. Lomas has striking blue eyes, Metzer has brown and one of those never opens fully. And tall. Metzer is one metre seventy at most, our man is nearer one ninety. That is Lomas on that plane, I am sure of it."

"Then the plan seems to be back on course," said the general. He picked up the receiver and spoke into it again.

"Are Faris and Saleem on board yet?" he asked his aide in the outer office. "They are. Good. Then tell air traffic control they can release the flight." He put down the telephone and turned to Khalid and Mundai.

"Two of my sons are on board the flight now and will track Lomas as far as they can before French or British immigration intercepts them. They are good sons, so we will have reliable intelligence from them on how our plan proceeds. Meanwhile I want you and Mundai to use your web of contacts to find this Günter Metzer and bring him here. I think it might be time to find out what he knows and to whom he tells it. Now go, both of you, and get some rest. You have done well, but now we must be patient. If the plan works and the Americans come to fight we will be ready and waiting for them. The streets of Baghdad will soon flow with the blood of the infidel and there will be the great victory for Islam we have awaited for, for so long. Praise be to Allah, and peace be upon him."

Father and son left together, into the Baghdad night. Khalid put his arm round his son's shoulder as they walked through the dark city streets. Mundai looked up at his father's sparkling teeth and the familiar grey walrus moustache and smiled.

"Even though, as you well know, Father, I don't drink alcohol, getting drunk on Scotch whisky with you sounds unusually attractive tonight," he said. "I'm going to hell anyway. So, take me with you to your club and Herr Metzer can keep 'till tomorrow."

Khalid laughed. "We can wait for the Americans together," he replied.

* * *

The charred remains of a man, found the following day in an alleyway behind one of Baghdad's most popular restaurants, were not confirmed to be those of Metzer until nearly four days later. At first there was no obvious cause of death other than burning. However, the subsequent post mortem revealed a massive disruption in an area around the sternum and extensive displacement of a single vertebra at the base of the neck which, without question, would have severed the spinal cord and caused death. Nothing on the body or in the body was found that could link the body to anything other than the German newspaper, *Hamburger Zeitung*, the newspaper for which Metzer reported. Spectral analysis of a notebook found near the body, in the embers of the fire, revealed only four lines of handwritten text and it was only a few words from these few lines that were legible enough to identifying Metzer as the author. Papers found in Metzer's room at the hotel and on which he had written, were made available for the forensics team to examine and compared with the writing from the notebook. It was immediately clear that each came from the same hand and the general was happy to conclude that it was Metzer who had perished so savagely in the fire.

It was therefore several days after the event that General Mahmud Hassan officially informed the paper in Germany of the unfortunate and unexplained circumstances surrounding the death of their former employee. He did so in the full knowledge that there would be questions asked in very secret places among the Western alliance, from Hamburg to Langley and then from Washington to London of course. The final piece of his plan would then slip into place.

But General Mahmud Hassan was a thorough man and he did not want to leave too much to chance. He walked away from the opened window of his office from which he had been gazing blankly, picked up the telephone receiver on his desk and pressed the green button.

"Ah, Mohamed, I wish to speak with his eminence Sir Geoffrey Fenton in London. Tell them it's important and of some urgency, national security and all that. On the secure line, if you would."

The general replaced the receiver, pressed the green button and its light went off with a dull click. He walked over to the opened window again, and smiled.

"You have had some of your best ideas looking out from this window," he said out loud to himself.

Chapter Eight

In France

At Charles de Galle they were met by more uniformed Air France staff. They helped Fabien on with her cashmere jacket and carried her case and bag for her. They even made several attempts to carry Eric's bag for him. Each polite request was met with a curt refusal. Lomas walked alongside Fabien and her little entourage who were bringing along her case and bag to the flight desk for her connecting flight to Rennes. The two attendants shook hands with her and wished both her and Lomas a safe and pleasant ongoing flight and quickly departed to administer their velvet gloved coddling to some other Air France clients in need of pampering.

"Well, the luxury ends here I guess," said Lomas after Fabien had checked in at the desk. Her suitcase had been whisked away, her documents checked and she was free to make her way to Departures.

"You're going straight on to London?" she asked, but already knew the answer.

"I am afraid I must," he replied, with genuine regret. "There may have been people on the plane still taking an interest in me and I don't want you to get mixed up in the problems my work has presented me with."

"I thought we had connected there for a while, I really did." She felt consumed by disappointment and Lomas could read it in her face and in the tone of her voice that had cracked when she spoke the words. He felt wretched.

She took a purse from her handbag and drew a card from it. "Here! If you are ever in near Saint Luc or Place de la Madeleine for that matter…" She stopped herself. There was so much more she wanted to say, but she knew she would be unable to continue with any semblance of dignity. She thrust the card at him. Lomas hung his head as he accepted it, holding the card with both hands. The printed card showed her name and addresses and telephone numbers on either side. She laid a soft hand gently on his bristly cheek, leaned forward and kissed the other. He took the hand from his face, kissed the palm of it and held it as if he would never let it go.

"Au revoir, Lomas," she whispered. He let her hand slip from his and she was gone.

She was walking away from him, through the departure gate and out of his sight. She was crying, he knew and he ached with anguish knowing he had caused her sadness. He had committed many crimes in the service to his country for which he had felt ashamed but at that moment he hated himself more than ever he had before. He stood riveted to the spot, head bowed and still looking at the card she had left with him. He could not bear it.

As she walked through the main concourse to the flight departure area drying her tears, she reminded herself how much she had missed her brother, Francoise. It was now just after eight o'clock which gave her an hour or more to wait for her flight's departure so she had time enough then to collect herself. Coffee and a brioche would help immensely she predicted and sat herself down in a corner of the first café she saw for breakfast. She found the strong black espresso to be expectedly reviving and the hot buttery brioche comforting somehow.

She was glad now she had just walked off like that. It was undoubtedly for the best he return to London but she chastised herself for being so impulsive, which was so unlike her usual restrained and reticent behaviour. She had misjudged him and felt a little foolish giving him her card and doubted now he would ever use it. She hoped though he had not thought her over dramatic.

It was when she was ordering her second coffee she saw him striding purposefully towards her table in the corner. He took her hands and pulled her up and kissed her on both cheeks. She hugged him close and the waiter taking her order was forced to take two paces backwards as Lomas swung her around in his arms.

"I'm sorry, old man, it's the Paris effect I think; seems to bring out the lover in one." Lomas set down his valise, ordered himself a coffee, Americano, and a croissant and sat down, across the table from Fabien so he could look at her.

"What are you doing?" Fabien enquired.

"I have a ticket to Rennes in my pocket and a sudden desire to be impulsive and take up your kind offer to visit your country home. Queen and country will wait, my dear Fabien."

The flight from Paris to Rennes took off on time at nine thirty. The flight was full and they were not able to sit together. There was a tense moment when a pedantic air steward insisted Lomas put his flight bag in the overhead locker, but Lomas had been adamant that it should stay with him and the steward relented, providing it was placed under his seat. Lomas agreed to the compromise. Feeling a little like a naughty school boy again he spent the hour they were in the air fidgeting in his seat trying to get a glimpse of Fabien when he could. For her part she waved and smiled at him several times to reward his interest but really she was in turmoil for she had not expected to feel like this.

Her car was a bright yellow Citroën 2CV. She drove from the airport, south. She avoided the autoroutes and stuck to country roads as much as possible. They chatted excitedly with each other and quickly developed an easy repartee. It was late October but the air still had some warmth in it, so they rolled the canvas roof back and Lomas sat with an elbow poking from the opened window and a hand on the back of Fabien's seat. He felt relaxed and happy in a way he had forgotten he could be. That was until he stole a glance over his shoulder to check the valise was still there safe on the back seat and reminded himself of the potentially horrendous danger it contained. At that moment though he felt no anger or vengeful rage towards those whom he considered had conspired to wipe out most of his family. He would all too soon have to make definite decisions concerning the final destination of the contents of that camera he carried hidden in the bag under his few clothes. *But not right now,* he thought, *not right now.* The French countryside was sliding slowly by. He could smell apples and manure. The trees had turned to yellows and reds and they shone on golden branches in the bright air. The sun was warm on him now at noon and all seemed right with the world. He wanted to forget all about Bessomthwaite 288 for a while, he could visit that particular problem at some later date.

Then suddenly later they were driving through a dark forest. The air was cooler then, as they moved through a tunnel of trees, over a long straight road towards the small circle of light where trees gave way eventually to the sun and bright sky again. Lomas did not fail to recognise that very thing was happening to him. He felt as if he was being drugged, remaining lucid, but drugged by the shear delight of being in sunlight after so many years struggling to find his way through a dense forest.

She was playing Chopin on her little in-car CD player and the subtle tinkling riffs of the piano exploded and diminished in perfect time and natural harmony with the clouds of orange leaves blown up in their wake. His once iron resolve was receding. This for him was a true moment of pure bliss, one he would always remember.

"I prefer to drive this way home, after working," she said breaking into the quiet that rested easily between them. "This drive gives me time to ease down and find myself again. It is this that keeps me sane I think sometimes. Often the patients take a toll on you. I get too involved, we all do. We wouldn't be human if we didn't, well I don't think so anyway. You get attached, no matter how many times we are told we must remain professional, unemotional and detached."

"It's working for me too," Lomas concurred.

"We could have been there by now if I used the autoroute," she explained.

"You're doing fine. Don't worry; I am enjoying this more than I could ever possibly explain to you."

"Are you hungry? It has gone noon. We should find somewhere soon for lunch if you are. The restaurants tend to fill very quickly. Lunch is the most important meal in France. I know a lovely restaurant we pass a bit further on."

"I'll leave it to you. Luncheon I agree would be welcome but, driving through this beautiful countryside as we are, I am feeding on other things."

She looked straight at him for a moment, and then returned her attention to the road ahead. "*C'est certain*, you are a deep, deep well of a man." In that moment she could see the magic working. Being there together, in that moment there with her, he was slowing down enough for him to take a breath. She wanted him unharmed but had never intended to help mend him. However, in putting him back together, perhaps she could begin to repair herself.

They spent two hours at luncheon. The small restaurant was packed and for all the time they were there eating, new arrivals were waiting patiently for a table to become available. The food was of course excellent and cheap at ten euros for five courses; soup, fish, meat, dessert, and cheeses. The wine was local and delicious but, after she had taken her first mouthful approvingly, Fabien diluted her wine with a little water, as she would have to drive again when they continued their journey. Lomas, however, did no such thing.

It was not until they returned to the car that he realised he had neglected to take proper care of the holdall and its precious and dangerous contents. The valise sat there on the back seat where he had left it unattended for the previous two hours. He knew he was becoming irresponsible and neglectful of his sworn duty. He noticed too that he was less concerned by his recklessness than he was with enjoying the full fury of happiness and contentment which now swirled around in him like an intoxicating cocktail and he just laughed at his forgetfulness.

As the open French countryside swept by and panned out either side of the deserted narrow roads along which they passed, an easy tranquillity and quietness began to settle between the two of them again. Fabien sang a little children's song, quietly, in French, as she drove, whilst Lomas was happy enough just to breathe in the air. Fragranced with the perfume of damp leaves and wet earth as it was, and redolent of the air in the Cumbrian hills of his boyhood, it was forgivable that he should remain unaware of the circle closing behind him as they approached the little village of Saint Luc de Vilaine.

"*Nous avons arrive!*" Fabien exclaimed in delight. She had pulled across the road to a shallow lay-by atop the ridge overlooking her village. "It is lovely, non?" she asked.

There, stretched out before him, Lomas saw the flint houses spread out away from the wide estuary of the river Ranche. A tall church bell tower rose up from the centre between the grey slated roofs. Just beyond the cottages that stood beside a full river, some boats were tied up at the quayside and men were unloading a few blue plastic crates filled with a variety of fish and crustaceans. The sun shone along the full river so that out towards the horizon it was difficult to see where exactly land finished and river, sea, and sky began. Before he could answer her, Fabien pointed excitedly towards the church spire.

"My cottage is just there."

"Oh yes, I see it."

"Oh, you are so silly, how could you know which it is. You have not been there yet."

"No, but I bet it is that one there, near the river with the blue shutters," he guessed.

"Yes, just so, but how could you know? Mine has the garden with the tall tulip tree, you see? Down there, look." She pointed towards the church again and then slapped him on the arm. "They all have blue shutters. Oh, you are having fun with me, no?"

"Oh every moment Fabien, every moment," he answered, truthfully.

They drove down the hill into the village, parked by the church and walked across the cobbles to a blue painted wooden door that opened straight onto the street. It sported a handsome metal knocker in the shape of a dolphin above a wide mouthed frog shaped letter-box. A plaster plaque displayed the number 29 and beneath the words, *Vingt-Neuf, Rue de l'Eglise*. There was a metal boot scraper beside the step and an ornamental goose with two goslings trailing behind her under one blue shuttered window. With no garden, no pavement either for that matter, Lomas wondered how long those goslings would have stayed with their mother if this was England.

The blue street door opened into a small, dark hallway. There were double doors of pale oak across the hallway which Fabien opened out onto a large, bright room. A carved wooden staircase, which wound itself around a central chimney, faced him as Lomas wandered from the hallway into the huge living space. She hung up her jacket on one of the coat hooks under the stairs, then took Eric's and hung it on the hook next to hers. Fabien kicked off her shoes and put on slippers. She told Lomas he could do the same and she would find him some slippers from her brother's things.

"Just dump the bags there under the coat-hooks," she told him. "We can sort those out later, after I have given you 'The Tour'."

Lomas removed his dusty desert shoes and placed them on his valise. He followed Fabien around her home, glad he had decided before leaving the hotel in Baghdad to put on the only pair of clean socks he had brought with him to Iraq.

The staircase and the bare brick chimney breast served to split the space almost in half which gave the impression of two distinctly separate yet adjoining rooms. On one side of the partition was the dining room, the second most important room in any French household and second only to the kitchen. A long refectory table, rustic carver chairs and a sideboard with a dresser top of the same old dark wood which displayed a full set of crockery in a modern plain design, all sat comfortably with the ambience of the exposed beams and brick construction. The varnished, flag-stoned floor was cold to Eric's stockinged feet but he noticed the hearth was set with kindling and logs for a fire if required. From that moment he was, without doubt, in France. What a lovely room, he thought, feeling at home immediately. He was pleased he had decided to make this small start in changing his life. Some light came into the room through the window which looked out onto the street and from two others in the long wall down the side of the cottage. They revealed a narrow lawn, a low hedge and the garden of the adjacent property. However, all the real brightness of the dining room came from beyond a wide arch that led into a small but well equipped kitchen. The far wall of the kitchen had been replaced completely with glass. Fabien opened the floor-to-ceiling folding glass doors and they stepped out onto a wide veranda. The glass panels moved noiselessly on their runners. Her veranda extended to the full width of the cottage and had wooden steps that descended to a wide lawn with herbaceous borders of lavender and rosemary, hibiscus and rhododendron. And there it was, at the end of a shingle path, the tulip tree she so prized.

"Let me just get you those slip-ons of Francoise's." She disappeared inside but was soon back and held a pair of brown leather clog-like slippers for him to wear.

"They should be big enough. They look about the same size as your boots. Come, let's sit for a moment," she said, leading him to the wooden bench built around the trunk of the large tree. "This is my favourite place to sit when I get back. I can think more clearly sitting under this tree. It is like being inside my own private cathedral under these branches."

They sat together under the branches of the tall tulip tree and the shadows grew longer as the sun slid down the orange sky into the dusk on the river behind and below them. Looking back up to the house, he saw the golden circular ends of many logs in the log store under the veranda. She saw many things that would now be done another day. It was getting cold now the sun was down and without meaning to she gently leaned into him. He sat quietly still, looking back up to the house but enjoying the mild frisson as she leant in on him. She continued to quietly look about her garden planning for the coming winter but she was leaning into him as she did so. Only gently, unnoticeably almost, but she leaned into him nonetheless.

If they were ever to ask themselves if their love had been real, it would be from this point they could have answered nothing other than yes. Neither of them had been looking in that direction, in fact both of them still had their own separate agenda. But there can be no doubt it started then and there, under that tall tulip tree.

They sat, at ease in one another's company and he listened to her explain how the cottage used to be two cottages, and how a retired English couple had spent years restoring and renovating the buildings. When they died the cottage came on the open market. She had redesigned the kitchen she told him. The eighteenth century range they built into the brick chimney-breast being the only original feature she thought might be worth keeping. "I use it all the time when I am here in the winter. Once the fire is lit I keep it in all the time, night and day. I even boil water in a kettle for making tea and use no electricity," she boasted.

Later, after she had shown him his sleeping quarters upstairs, Fabien lit a small fire in the hearth of the big sitting room. This room was comfortable and still warm from the afternoon sun which had streamed in through the wide expanse of panelled glass that ranged across the western end of the room. Although closed now these panels could be folded back like a concertina as could the windows in her kitchen, she explained, opening onto the veranda and the garden beyond.

They had agreed on a light supper, after such a filling lunch. She made a soup from fresh vegetables and herbs from her garden, and a wonderful cheese and tomato omelette that hinted only at the delicate flavours of parsley and chives. Eric opened a second bottle of wine, this time a dry red Pissotte from the Vendee. He tasted it and approved.

"Tastes expensive," he said.

"Not at all, but it is a lovely boutique wine. I found it in a supermarket for only six euros a bottle last year when I was in the Vendee. It comes from a small vineyard near Vouvant. See the two interwoven hearts on the bottle? It is the emblem of the department du Vendee. They only make a small amount each year. I must remember to get some more before it becomes more popular and too expensive." They chatted together enjoying the wine and each other's company as if they had been old friends and were catching up, just now meeting again after a long time.

Rather than use the dining room, Eric had suggested a more informal approach to the evening, so they sat on the floor, on huge cushions from the sofas, around a large heavy coffee table. There was a television under the stairs facing them but there was music to provide an appropriate background for their relaxed conversation whilst eating, and drinking the wine. In fading light they watched the fire leaping and flickering until it became dark outside. Fabien switched on low lighters for the room, a couple of table lamps and a scented candle in one of the side windows that faced south, which only added to the room's ambience.

"What is this music?" he asked, only just noticing it for the first time. "I really like it."

"It's Moby, his new album, Play," she replied. "Have you heard of him? He is Herman Melville's great grandson or something; the author of *Moby Dick*."

"Arh yes! *Moby Dick*. Now I come to think on it, Captain Ahab and I have a good deal in common. I too have been a driven man. A man so driven it has prevented me from seeing what has actually been happening. It cost him his life in the end, didn't it. Well call me Ishmael if you like but that's not going to happen to me. I intend to resign completely from the service."

"Is it because of what you found out in the desert?" she asked, naively.

He did not answer her. A persistent fly had been circling round their food while they were talking, now Lomas slowly reached for the linen napkin beside his empty plate. He flicked it out at the intruder and the tip cracked. He allowed himself a quick smile of self-satisfaction as the fly fell to the floor quite dead.

"Resign? But you enjoy killing don't you, I see it in your eyes." It was not a question.

"Not enjoy, no. With practice I have become very good at it. It is perhaps a sense of pride you see, in doing a job well, to the best of one's ability. No more than that; now anyway."

"Is that what you do for the British government?" she asked.

He found himself wanting to confide in her.

"I have done," he replied.

She waited for him to continue.

"I mean I used to. You see I have been brought up and educated to believe it is my duty to make a difference and believed that this difference was for the defence of my home and family. Gradually all this has been taken away from me. All I have been left with is a feeling of revulsion at the terrible things I have done and the manner in which I did them. It was as though I knew, or rather, convinced I was doing the right thing. That almost makes it worse. What I discovered in the desert has shown me there are people at home who care nothing of right and wrong, and have used me as their instrument of death, like a marionette dancing on the end of their strings. Like Gregory Peck as, Captain Ahab, was inescapably bound to the whale he hunted, I am dragged down into the depths of evil by the great white whale I call loyalty and duty. Guilt, that's really what I found in the desert, not some old WMD that has wiped out my entire family. My own guilt, that's what I found. I have never felt guilty before for any of the things I have had to do, but I suddenly feel wretched and in need of redemption."

She reached out and placed her warm hand on his forearm.

"If you look hard enough you'll see there are no real ties to bind you to that life. Leaving that life behind may be in itself your redemption. As a soldier for your country you are expected to do dangerous and violent things. Was it your fault that Iraq invaded Kuwait? Or was it your fault that the junta in Buenos Aries decided to invade the Malvinas? No, but as a soldier you have to fulfil your duty." She hoped what she was intending to explain was helping, but he showed no evidence that it was. "I don't want to know too many of your secrets. You may have to kill *me* if you did," she added.

"I felt angry and vengeful yesterday and would not have confided to you any details of my malevolent past solely for my own protection, now I do because with guilt comes shame. I am ashamed of my past actions and want you to view me in the best light possible. Through you I see my salvation. Were it not for you bringing me here, and being here with me now I would still be in such turmoil. I should have been back to face that destiny which has been preordained almost for me by the people who really pull my strings, the corrupt puppeteers. I can't remember when I have felt so relaxed anywhere, or with anyone. I can talk freely with you. 'Tis Kismet Hardy', but a different fate to that which I was prescribed I believe."

They sat quietly for awhile, the fire crackling in the grate providing a comforting backing track.

"May I stay a couple of days?" he asked, suddenly. "There is something necessary for me to do in London but I need a little time to work out how. Is that okay? Two, three days, no more. I need to go back in a state of calm, not in a state of grace."

"I am so glad you feel comfortable here." She got up and began clearing the bowls and plates from the table. "Now you appear to have given up any intention to murder me in my sleep, you can of course stay as long as you wish." They both laughed.

"Here, I'll help." He picked up the glasses and the two empty wine bottles and followed her out to the kitchen. "I am bushed, I think I'll turn in if that's okay."

She put the dirty crockery on the heavy oak kitchen table and as he reached forward to put the glasses and bottle down she turned and held him.

"I hope I am in some way part of this new perspective you have to your life," she whispered.

"Indeed you are, Fabien. I feel like I've been here before, almost like I belong. 'Kismet, Hardy'."

"Don't keep calling me Hardy," she joked breathlessly and kissed him full on the mouth.

She wanted him. She wanted him right then and forever. She let go of the past she had so long endured and grasped her unknown future with total ecstasy.

Chapter Nine

An Epiphany

When he woke, Lomas was alone in the bed they had shared after yet another night of love making. She had gone to get bread from the depository. He showered and dressed and as he had done on the previous mornings he checked in his bag that the camera was still there. It had grown to the size of an elephant now and he knew its implications could not be ignored any longer, no matter how pleasant things had turned out for him just recently.

From the trunk that had belonged to her late brother, Fabien had found some warm clothes for him that fitted and Eric had found her the first morning about to put them into his bag. She seemed embarrassed but he had told her he had no qualms about wearing a dead man's clothes, as he had been required to do that very thing many times before. So he had come down to the breakfast table in the kitchen that first morning looking very smart and very French. The broken debris from their outburst of passion had been cleared away but there remained still lodged in his thoughts the memory of it. Each time he had entered the kitchen since that first night an enriching frisson of sensual delight would pass through him as he recalled it and he would be lifted from the terrors of his troubled sleep, but not today. Today for good reason he remained gloomy.

The nightmares of his earlier life that filled his sleep with the stilled and silent faces of those he had killed were not at once terrorising to him. It was more as if those events replayed continually throughout his subconscious like a film, rather than real events remembered. He had always felt detached, as if he was watching a loop of newsreel over and over, but on occasions he would suddenly recognise the reality of what he was and what he had done to those people. It was always the unexpected suddenness of this which terrorised him most. But it was not even this that blackened his mood.

He and Fabien, while languishing in a blissful pool of post coital ecstasy the previous evening, had confessed their secret motives to each other; Lomas, from a desire to begin as he intended to continue, in honesty and with Fabien, in the hope she could prevent London being laid to waste. But what Fabien had told him seemed to have a profound effect on Lomas and he had remained quiet and sullen.

He could see that she had become frightened of him so he had attempted to reassure her he could not harm her and that he was working out how he could prove his feelings for her.

Eric poured himself a cup of coffee and took it out with him onto the veranda. He sat looking out over the garden and down towards the river below it. He hoped the fresh brackish air would snap him out of his ill-temper. Lomas could not see the kelp, but he knew it were there. As the falling tide exposed more of the salt marsh beyond the bend in the river he could smell it in the wind. When he was a child his mother had used iodine to disinfect his scrapes and grazes. The antiseptic would leave an orange and pungent stain on his skin; a visible, tangible indicator of pain and injury. The seaweed had a similar smell to those dressings and he thought again about the mother with whom he had spent so little time. Where was the orange stain for that injury? When he looked for the wounds causing his pain he was never able to expose them, but that did not mean there were none there. He suspected there were very many and up to now he had been forced to keep them well hidden. He had no orange marker for them.

There was a steady breeze that morning, it plucked at the wire stays of the bigger yachts bobbing at their moorings in the river and it hummed in the rigging of the smaller tipped-over sailing boats mud-bound halfway out into the main channel. A small formation of turnstones glided down the stiff air to suddenly turn up and into it again. Then, drifting down with wings high above their heads, their bodies and feet dangling, they gently dropped to the very edge of the water margin again, but a little further down river. Immediately they began to dip and step and prick and prod for a meagre meal of tiny stranded waterborne animals. An oystercatcher Lomas had spotted there on the mud bank seemed to view these enthusiastic new arrivals on its particular stretch of mud with a degree of disdain. The turnstones darted and scuttled around him, blissfully unaware of this scorn. The bigger bird stood alone in his contempt, aloof and elegant in his black and white dinner jacket. He stood with the bright orange baton of his beak poised, like that of a long suffering conductor forced by circumstance to preside over an agitated and unruly orchestra of unheeding naughty children. Regally the oyster catcher retained his haughty calmness amid these frenetic little interlopers, unmoved by their furious foraging. Even as his shadow was becoming fainter and the reflection of him too faded gradually in the wet grey silt as it slowly dried out, the oyster catcher seemed not to notice the darker clouds which were blowing in over the pale morning sun. The oyster catcher remained, as do all creatures other than man himself, unconcerned by the meaning of his existence and the passing of time and tides.

Lomas had no need to contemplate too long to draw a parallel. He had never questioned the reasons for his blind acceptance of his own life and the way it had been, nor had he ever even attempted to look beyond a blinkered adherence to duty before?

When a man breaks it rarely shows. There is certainly no iodine highlighter for this type of damage, nor is there for the many other injuries that have caused the corrosion of his soul. He can continue to function on many levels of his existence. He can work, he can think, he can be funny, he can be cruel, he can pretend to love. But when a man really goes, this all changes: everything changes. Everything changes but he does not realise it. He can pretend to work, he can pretend he can think, he can even pretend to be funny, but he can't be cruel anymore, not really cruel. Cruelty requires some degree of malicious intent and he has none left.

As Lomas can see now for himself, he could still kill and still do cruel things, even to those close to him, but it has become just something he does. These acts would have no intent attached to them, they would merely be necessary. And he can't pretend to love anymore because it is now, when love comes to him without any pretence, that he begins to suspect that he has gone and has been gone for some time. A man looks back over his life thinking he can pinpoint where and when he broke, but a single moment very rarely shows up, it is more usually a result of slow erosion.

But it is suddenly that this happens to Eric; finally. When true love comes to him as it has, his whole life becomes uncloaked by the truth of it. It is undoubtedly true that he has been broken and repaired so many times before just so he could stand tall again and carry on. It is a duty he has been taught to owe himself that has forced him to continue for so long. Being a man, being a hard man, being the one human being life has been unable to humble and it is this which finally gives way. What value has duty when the value of loyalty is abused by those who demand it? Just as a piece of metal continually folded backwards and forwards will eventually snap, the capacity of a man to carry on being hurt and broken by life fails. His previous life is like a short length of elastic he at first only had to hold lightly between his thumb and forefinger. Then as this length of elastic is stretched out, down the years, the tension becomes too great for him to hold onto it any longer, the elastic slips from his grip and twang, the man is adrift.

The swift air was barely less than constant in its power but even so, when the wind speed eased momentarily, stutteringly a single stay slapped up against one of the masts in the estuary and seemed to mimic the tick-tock-tick of an old clock and Lomas knew that time for him had finally run out; as quickly as the tide. So it was then, at that moment standing on the wide veranda of Fabien's house looking out across the narrow spit of mud and shingle between the kelp beds and the ocean, that Eric really understood what he must do. The elastic had finally slipped from between his fingers. He no longer felt bound by duty to defend a philosophy that had caused the deaths of his parents and then his wife and sons. He understood now something he had really always known: that there was a great evil in the world of which he had been a part and that it is the ambivalence of the good which only serves to inspire daring in those who are evil. A lifetime of wounds, which had prevented him from seeing the true nature of his work and which he had been able to hide away so well, were now demanding to be cleansed.

Being there in Brittany with Fabien for those few wonderful days had helped Lomas to see how his mettle had been twisted once too often and how the memory of his mother's tender care of him when he was a boy, borne back to him on the wind from the iodine scented kelp on the river, had set loose his grip on the life he had led and the person he had been before. He breathed in the fresh salty air that swept insistently round that curve in the river Rance knowing he had to act and act soon, before his resolve turned to complete acceptance of the happiness which he had walked into so unexpectedly.

He left that morning. It didn't take him long to pack his few things. He had left the majority of his effects in Iraq anyway. He left a note for Fabien to find when she returned from the market. It read:

My dearest darling,

I can't tell you how much you have helped me recover from the ten years of torture I have endured. We are a real thing you and I. With Katherine I abused the love and loyalty she gave me and I have no intention of repeating this failure. You deserve more.

I have to go back to England, to finally put an end to my old life. I have no idea how this will end, but know this is something I must do. I will not be free of it if I do not.

If you and I are to have any chance of happiness I must do this. You do see my darling, don't you? I love you, and I will return. Then we can make a life together you and me, if you'll still have me.

Eric.

He folded the paper, took an envelope from the drawer of the old oak dresser where he had found pen and paper, slipped his missive into the envelope and sealed it. On the front he scrawled *Fabien* and propped it up on the kitchen table against the glass vase of chrysanthemums she had picked before leaving for market. He breathed in the deep pungent fragrance of the colourful bouquet so he could fix the scent of the flowers in his mind. He wanted to become haunted by it, in the same way the smell of kelp and sometimes hyacinths haunted him. He wanted to be here always if he could.

How different this leaving was from the one he had planned. It was the mention of her home near Saint Malo that had prompted him to make the first move towards her, serious move that is. He had supposed and even imagined a liaison of convenience with Fabien, using her to escape the Iraqi security service and assist in his return to England via the Channel Islands. He had never left such a loose end like this before, but now he loved her, what else could he do? This warm and vital woman meant everything to him. Metzer's killing had been necessary in maintaining his cover for as long as possible, but he cringed now as he recalled just how coldly he had planned Fabien's death. Saint Malo was certainly where he was headed, but he did so now with the heaviest of hearts.

He gripped the handles of his valise and passed a long last glance over the room, packing in every detail he could take with him to remind him of this wonderful place and his epiphany; the fire flickering inside the wide range, the pots and pans hanging from racks above the stove. The stone jars filled with strong rough cider and country wine, red as blood. Smaller ones with vinegars and oils for cooking. A large wedge of yellow cheese he noticed was left out on the side dresser in the air to mature, and the remnants of a loaf of bread that sat on end on the breadboard in a sea of crumbs. It was stale no doubt and was probably what had sent Fabien out for fresh baguettes and a new loaf from the *boulangerie*.

He passed a hand along the oak table where they had sat eating, drinking wine, and talking late into the night. His hand rested on the spot to where he had gently lifted her, and the moment replayed in his mind. Plates and glasses had been swept out of the way and smashed onto the cold stone floor; collateral damage in the explosion of their pent up desire for one another. Only a vase of red and yellow chrysanthemums reflecting in the dull patina of the old wood remained on the table. As he propped the letter up against the flower vase he tried to remember who it was had started it off.

It had been he who carefully picked open a button at the front of her blouse but it was she who laughed and then kissed him and so it was that each button he unfastened, slowly and deliberately, released yet another square centimetre of her soft quivering flesh. It was he who cupped a hand gently under each of her breasts and like small birds, soft and trembling they rested in his palms, each nipple hard as a frozen raspberry, pert and red and ready. But it was she who then placed her hands behind his head and pulled his mouth onto hers. It was her darting tongue that found his, and it was her arms then that held them together, tightly. It was she who wore nothing under her thin skirt and she who pressed herself onto him so he could feel her prickly warmth through his cotton trousers. It was he who, stepping out of these and his Calvin Kleins, had lifted her up onto the table by her buttocks and it was he who had swept the table clear of crockery and cutlery that crashed and clattered onto the floor beside the table, but it was she who allowed her legs to part and dangle across his forearms as he lifted her up onto the table.

Her warmth was now a fluid slippery warmth against him. and it flowed and pulsed like a tidal surge through them both. He saw the brief flicker of surprise rise fleetingly in her face and then her eyes slowly close as the trance of ecstasy overwhelmed her. Her legs swung from his arms, like those of a lifeless doll's, moving only as a counter rhythm to his gentle thrusts. One dainty shoe slipped slowly from her swinging foot and toppled unnoticed to lie with the broken pieces of clay and glass strewn across the stone floor.

He broke free from the memory and closed the door behind him. This was his new day, the day he would begin his renaissance; renaissance not through retaliation, retribution or revenge, but through restoration and redemption. As he stepped out into the bright afternoon he promised himself he would return and live a different life, a blissful life with Fabien. All he needed to do to fulfil this promise was to survive the next few days.

He felt confident of success as he walked along the old quay, past the tied-up fishing boats. The pale sun emerged momentarily and glinted in the glass balls which hung from high wide fishing nets draped across the fronts of the fishermen's cottages. He decided to go up the hill away from the river and the market and avoid any chance of seeing Fabien returning. Leaving like this was hard enough. He could not imagine the pain of trying to explain everything to her and seeing her reaction. Up past the better of the two auberge in the village he walked and into the open country behind the church of Our Lady of Gethsemane. Over the brow of the hill he went and down the narrow lane between the high stone-built walls towards the railway station and a train to Saint Malo. Eventually a ferry would take him to the channel island of Guernsey and finally another to the coast of England, where he hoped to pass unnoticed into obscurity.

Fabien returned from the market a while later and found his letter. She was a little surprised by his sudden departure, but managed to suppress her disappointment. She pulled the mobile phone from her bag and began a text message. She started in French then changed her mind: English seemed a language better suited to *double entendre* than either Arabic or French. The message read: "*Your fish is believed heading for Thames area this morning. Delivery on track, therefore expect settlement of our account soonest.*" She pressed send and then sat down with a large glass of a very good white wine and a feeling of excited anticipation. Any satisfaction she may have expected she would feel was tinged now with more than a modicum of regret that he had gone and might never return.

Chapter Ten

In with the Minister

"Ah, Sir Geoffrey, here you are," said the minister, calmly, though slightly startled. "Leave us, Hoskins, we'll continue this, this afternoon."

"Of course, Minister," his secretary replied. She had been taking notes when Fenton knocked and entered the office, expected but unannounced. She immediately stood, straightened her tight knee-length black skirt and left them.

"And tell Dawson would you, if he is at his desk that is, no calls until Sir Geoffrey and I have finished. Now, what seems to be the trouble, old boy? You're looking rather perplexed," he asked in a friendly but mocking tone. The two men sat down opposite one another across a broad red tooled-leather topped desk. They both watched Ms Hoskins leave the room, as if they might be required later to give marks out of ten for artistic interpretation. Ms Hoskins, for her part, was not unaware of their attentions. "Lovely girl, and good at her job too," added the minister appreciatively, when she had eventually closed the door.

Sir Geoffrey Fenton was sure Ms Hoskins was competent in every department, but said nothing to support this supposition. On the wall behind the minister hung a full-length portrait of Queen Elizabeth 1, painted by Hans Holbein the "even younger". Completed in 1592 when all of Western Europe was celebrating the first centenary of Columbus's discovery of The Americas, it portrayed an aging queen who had tired of men and their infidelities. Good Queen Bess appeared to Fenton at that moment to have fixed her downward stare upon the minister himself. Although Fenton had been in this office many times before and seen several different ministers sitting in front of that portrait, he had never really noticed until this day the queen's expression, which had become to him just then so obviously one of disapproval and distain. Previous meetings with the minister generally, considering the importance of their positions and the difficult decisions they were expected to make whenever they met, surprisingly had always been conducted in an atmosphere of pleasant good humour. However, this morning Fenton knew there would be little time for levity, and he wanted to get quickly to the point. Besides which, it was common knowledge throughout Westminster that the minister and Ms Hoskins played together after school and what ever Fenton had said at that moment would have sounded condescending at best, or at worst like smutty innuendo. So Fenton thought better of making any comment regarding Ms Hoskins' many and considerable attributes.

The minister however took this momentary silence to be a rebuff and proceeded to make his displeasure apparent. The minister was well known for his feigned tetchiness, even when in good humour. He believed it lent a modicum more of menace to his otherwise benevolent personality. The minister suspected, correctly too, that he was not going to like what he was about to hear.

"So, get on with it then. What is it that is so urgent my early morning schedule has to be disrupted?" he asked, in a tone more brusque than Fenton liked or indeed was used to. But that was no bad thing for his purpose Fenton thought. He needed the minister engaged and focused on what he was about to be told. The minister was one of the new breed of politicians. In it for the salary rather than to fulfil an inherent duty as a servant of society. In it for the power, but not the responsibility. Fenton knew this minister would be the least likely to resign over a matter of principle than any minister under whom he had served before; but Fenton, for his part, worked well with this man. He found the minister to be a clever and wise man, not always both at the same time it was true, but Fenton had always thought that with a little encouragement, a little flattery perhaps, the Minister could be persuaded to do the right thing at the right time, as long as in doing so his office as minister was not directly threatened.

Sir Geoffrey had once compared the position of Secret Services Minister to that of a Premiership football team manager, whose work goes on in between the players' dressing room and the boardroom. The individual who, when too many goals are scored against the team, is the one left out on his own. However, even though Fenton understood he would be hard pushed to find any government colleague who would describe this minister as a team player and even with the certainty that any loyalty or trust shown on his part probably would not be reciprocated, Fenton had promised himself to give this man with the impossible job his total confidence and respect. For all his short comings Fenton liked the minister, which was why he sat there now before him and a discerning queen, about to put him well and truly in the picture. It had also occurred to Fenton of course that now, the minister could not at a later date distance himself completely from all the fallout by denying this initial meeting and briefing ever occurred. Dawson, the receptionist who had just waved him straight through to the minister's office, Sir Geoffrey knew was Service and could be relied upon if things got messy.

"We have a possible internal security problem, Minister. My department are still assessing the situation, but I thought you should know of it, before COBRA has to be involved."

"That serious?" questioned the minister.

"Possibly, yes. Potentially circumstances could change very quickly on this one. I thought we needed to look at one another's cards before we play out this particular hand," Fenton confided.

"Oh, that serious, best have a snifter then, eh? What do you drink, old man?" The minister made to get up from behind his desk. For his own part the minister had taken to Sir Geoffrey too, from their very first meeting, and believed he could rely on Fenton to provide him with accurate, strategic information with no side or swerve attached to it. It was the reason he had total respect for Fenton's opinion and valued his advice. Truth to be told, the minister hoped Fenton felt the same towards him but it was not, the minister knew, a necessity. After all it was his scrawny secondary modern neck alone that had been placed on this particular block by the PM. It had not been long after the promotion, finally achieving his personal goal to become a government minister before he was forty, when he began to realise just how much of a poisoned chalice this new post really was to be. He held dominion over many hundreds of highly trained and dedicated personnel whose sole purpose was to keep secrets. He was astute and clever enough, he felt, to keep their secretive and covert status not merely monitored but under some semblance of control, modern media politics demanded that this was so; or so the PM had told him. He knew that if anything went horribly wrong there would be a polite request from Downing Street for him to seriously consider spending more time with his family and that was not an ambition he currently held.

"Oh no, thank you. Far too early for me, Minister, but you might need one yourself," Fenton replied.

The minister remained seated. "No, let me hear what you have to say first," he said, with irritated concern.

"Our old friend from Baghdad has been on the blower, late last night."

"I assume you refer to Mahmud Hassan," the minister snapped.

"Indeed, Minister, I do. He seems to be concerned that one of my team has discovered a substantial amount of the pernicious toxin, Bessomthwaite 288, stockpiled in the southern desert near Kabala. You may remember a memo from Hans Blixe's team co-ordinator a few months ago, assuring us that all our old stuff had been destroyed after Kuwait."

"Yes, it would be a little embarrassing to us if it were to come to light that Saddam has some of this stashed away somewhere, I can see that. So what, there's some been found by one of your agents? So long as the UN team are kept away from it there's no harm done, is there? Saddam's not likely to go and use it, is he? He is, by all the reports from Baghdad and Washington: 'destroying WMDs quicker than we can find them.' That is the latest spin in the media, is that not so?"

"Yes, Minister. All you have said is true. However, there is a further complication in that our agent has managed to smuggle two vials of Bessomthwaite 288 out of Iraq and is heading for London with it in his pocket, we think." Fenton paused before continuing. The minister had plunged suddenly, deeply, into thought and said nothing. Elizabeth Regina also remained silent behind him; intent in her indignation.

"Good God, man. What makes you think that?" asked the minister, visibly shaken.

"I believe he'll come for me, kill me and then kill himself by releasing the pathogen where it will do the most damage and have the greatest effect."

The minister looked puzzled. "Why?" he asked. "He's one of yours isn't he?"

"Oh yes you could say he's one of mine," Fenton cryptically replied. "He has never been told exactly how his wife and children died. For operational reasons it was considered unhelpful to give him all the information at once. He reacted badly enough six months ago when the Iraqi government allowed the names to be released of those killed at Kabala compound. For ten years they had been listed by the Iraqis as missing presumed killed. I couldn't tell him it was probably our bombs that killed his family, although I am sure he had worked that out for himself and now this. I should have told him about the Bessomthwaite 288 when their names were eventually sent to us as among those killed. I think he has all along thought it was something nasty, just because of the delay in publishing the list of those killed. I would imagine he is a bit angry now. Wouldn't you be?"

"This is a bloody mess, Fenton, a right royal bloody catastrophe," stormed the minister losing his composure completely. "We must seal all the ports and airports, find him and take him out, liquidate him or whatever you people do. Do you hear me?" he raged.

"He's already in the country, we just don't know where yet."

"Oh fucking excellent, just fucking perfect."

"Look, all of this can be contained by my department I believe, if I am given a free hand," Sir Geoffrey assured him. "Apart from two major stumbling blocks."

The minister, who was at last beginning to realise the necessity for this unscheduled early morning meeting, guessed Fenton was coming to the crux of the matter. He calmed down somewhat and was beginning to understand this might be a problem he should stand well away from. He shifted nervously in his chair behind the desk and Fenton noticed this. Before the minister could speak, Sir Geoffrey continued.

"Firstly: we have not had any contact with this agent since he supposedly left for Iraq. We have not been able as yet to track him. He has not used his mobile phone or credit cards since he was last seen in Baghdad. Mahmud Hassan has had men tracking him. They lost him in the airport in Paris but picked up another trace in Brittany. According to Hassan our man sailed to Guernsey via St Malo yesterday and boarded a Seacat bound for Weymouth yesterday afternoon. Two Iraqi nationals were picked up in Guernsey yesterday. We are interviewing them now. So at this moment I have only General Hassan's assurance that this is not just a scenario on his wish list. How well this would suit them though if all this were found to be true. Our own agent, turned hostile, allowed back into this country with enough toxin to wipe out Greater London."

"Excuse me, Sir Geoffrey, what exactly was this agent going to do in Iraq? I understood all our assets there were embedded in the area years ago," the minister interrupted, finally.

"They are. They were. He went to see their grave. His wife and twin sons were captured in Kuwait and taken to Kabala when Operation Desert Storm began. His wife and two sons, along with others, were being used by Saddam as human shields at the Kabala compound. It was most tragic."

"Oh I see, yes I remember. The Iraqis opened up the grave site and gave out the names only six months ago," said the minister, remembering a number of tricky moments with the PM over the issue. However, he appeared to be genuinely moved. "Tragic, really tragic," he mumbled but then recovered himself.

"Nevertheless, the real tragedy here is that you sent him out there, in the first place. What were you thinking?" Already the minister was starting to dig himself an escape tunnel.

"I didn't send him; he went of his own volition, and under his own steam. There would have been little I could have done to stop him anyway, even if he had been operational, which he wasn't. I suspended him from duty following the announcement of the victims' names. He took it very badly."

"Yes, I read the report. So he wasn't there officially at all then was he?" The minister made a mental note of this then tried a different tack.

"But they may well have captured your man and if they are torturing him we should assume he will blow our whole network in Iraq and possibly the entire region, right? You should have stopped him going there," insisted the Minister.

"That possibility still exists," said Fenton, ignoring the minister's accusation. "If General Hassan has him imprisoned and is torturing him, he is presenting us with this as a ruse merely to gain a bit more time to neutralise those embedded agents before we officially request the return of our man. But I doubt that very much, we have had no concrete indication that any of our remaining assets over there have been touched," Fenton reassured him.

"So he's either in some Baghdad dungeon with electrodes attached to his scrotum, or on his way here to release a mini Armageddon, here in the capital. Great, sounds like we're screwed what ever." The minister seemed reconciled for a moment to his impending fate.

"Cheer up, Minister; it is more than likely neither are the case. I am certain he is not being held in Iraq. The Iraqis have seemed particularly unwilling to be seen to impede anyone working with the UN inspection teams. It was for that reason I asked you, two weeks ago, to issue him with necessary paperwork to get him onto one of those UN WMD inspection teams. I knew the Iraqis wouldn't dare touch him then," Fenton said, assuredly. "The ISS would know who he was really of course, but all his paperwork says UN, making him as untouchable as a diplomatic pouch."

"Very clever of you," the minister conceded. "Ah yes, Eric Lomas wasn't it? Didn't his parents have something to do with bio-chemical weapons too, I seem to recall? I remember now reading the report you sent at the time. Dr Philip Lomas and his wife, Ilyana, Russian wasn't she?" he asked.

"No, Hungarian, Minister," said Fenton, quickly making the distinction. "She was educated in Moscow after the war, and returned to Hungary to continue her research. She was a brilliant bio-chemist, top of her field apparently. I was one of the team sent in to extract her from Budapest in 1960, after the Russian invasion." It was unlike Fenton to give any personal information that was not demanded but, he felt the minister needed reminding that Fenton in the past had himself been a field operative and not a man with whom one would want to take too many liberties.

"Really, I didn't know that. They were both killed, weren't they? Some dreadful accident or some such, wasn't it?" the minister continued probing.

"She died, at the laboratory, yes. But he, Dr Philip Lomas shot himself not long after."

Fenton showed no emotion. He had found that a poker face was essential in these games he and the minister played.

"Couldn't live without her I suppose," said the minister, wistfully. "He must have loved her so much, I guess. That's quite touching actually, isn't it? Don't you think?" The minister required an answer.

"Who can say?" Fenton replied.

"He's had a bad run of luck; family wise that is, this fellow of yours. Seems to have been a good agent though, nothing ever comes back to bite."

"He is my best man; I would not want to lose him." Sir Geoffrey Fenton expressed a great deal of pride in saying so.

"Have you ever loved a woman like that? I don't mean safe, like with your wife, I mean out of control, fierce passion that consumes even your instincts of self-preservation. Must be unbelievably exhilarating." Fortunately, this time the minister was not looking for an answer, his thoughts had drifted momentarily to Ms Hoskins. Behind him, Elizabeth Tudor's frowning countenance had not softened in the slightest.

"Secondly," Fenton urged, attempting to regain the Minister's attention, "General Hassan has the incinerated remains of a German journalist he suspects has been killed by our man. This journalist, one Günter Metzer, turns out to be none other than Peter Hansen, CIA. The Iraqis suspect that he and our man were working together, but I doubt that very much. Eric always works alone."

"Oh God no, the Americans aren't mixed up in this, are they?"

"Not yet they are not. I am guessing Peter Hansen, alias Günter Metzer, was killed by our man to keep the Americans out of this long enough to leave the field clear for his own play. This is why I am here. You still have a position of believable deniability. I have told you all I can at the moment and we should meet no more until this is resolved. You can always reach me by the other conduits if necessary but I would not advise it. What I have told you so far is pure conjecture, and from an unsubstantiated source. If you are happy to keep the Yanks off our backs and let us deal with it in house, you have no need to get anymore closely involved, unless of course you feel the need to, Minister." Fenton was insistent.

"Oh no. No, I agree. If the Americans find out we have found our own bio-weapons in Iraq, they won't care about any political fallout over here, they are just waiting for any excuse to wade into Saddam and want to drag us into it with them."

"That's what I like about you, Minister, the speed with which you can grasp the nub of a situation and its political subtleties." It was like stroking a cat, and the minister responded in just the way Fenton hoped he would.

"I see now the government has been placed on the horns of a dilemma," the minister commented, reflectively. "The Government's position, Fenton, off the record of course, is that a war in Iraq is not one that can be easily won. And there is no way the country as a whole will agree to a war with Saddam, even though everyone knows what a monster he is. That's why the British Government has taken the stance that we will back American intervention in Iraq, only if WMDs are found. If this gets to the Americans we will have to back the Yanks and announce to the world, we know for certain there are WMDs in Iraq. But then to prove this intelligence correct the prime minister will have to admit publicly, publicly mind you, that these weapons are made using a substance made here, a substance banned by all recent treaties signed by the United Nations. But we thought, to let the most dangerous despot in history have some to try out on his neighbours, was a good idea." The minister, was standing and ranting again, red-faced and banging his hands on the desk.

"Got it in one," Fenton replied.

"You are confident of the veracity of this intelligence?" the minister asked, calm again.

"As much as one can be. Call it instinct, but I advise we act on the intelligence we have as if it were fact until we can prove it is fantasy," said Fenton.

"The PM should be advised about this straightaway," suggested the minister, in an attempt to shore up his partly dug escape tunnel. He leant forward for the phone on his desk.

"Are you sure that's prudent, at this stage?" advised Sir Geoffrey. "Believable deniability don't forget. Maybe, when 'The situation has been dealt with, and resolved', would be better timing. Isn't that what all PMs want, solutions not problems?"

"You are right, of course." The minister sat back in his chair and fixed Sir Geoffrey with a stare. "Find him before he can show any proof, and more importantly before I am forced to abandon my position of believable deniability for one of deniable believability." He was quiet voiced and completely calm again, menacing. "I am going to leave our response to this threat entirely to your discretion, for the moment. But at all costs he must be found and stopped. Am I making myself clear? Found and stopped. No half measures, no slip ups. If so much as a whisper of this leaks out, it could herald the fall of the Government? That fact may not be of great concern to you personally I know, Sir Geoffrey, given your impartiality as an unelected public servant, but I would consider it my business, in the event, to make it your concern. There are committees, such as the Honour Forfeitures Committee, over which I have more than a little sway. Failure is not an option because the repercussions from failure here will be seismic." The minister's voice had now attracted a sinister tone which was far more effective than the tetchy act ever was, as this was genuine. "This must be dealt with quickly and quietly. Any links back to your department must be cut, terminated. Do I make myself absolutely clear? If I am the one telling Washington 'We have no knowledge,' there must be no misunderstanding between us. I mean, no leakage and all links to the department terminated as if none existed. I will be the one to inform the PM when, and only when, this situation, true or imagined, has been normalised. Do we understand each other?"

"You just keep the CIA away from me and leave us to do our work and I anticipate a satisfactory solution to this present problem. However, let me remind you, Minister, of my curriculum vitae and just how in serving the country as a field operative I have earned the honours my country has bestowed upon me. You would have to tear each one, including the knighthood from my bleeding fingertips with your dying hands, Minister, make no mistake." Fenton's gaze never faltered, his face emotionless.

"Are you threatening me, old boy?" the minister asked, somewhat taken aback.

"No more than you are me, old boy," mimicked Fenton. "I will not allow my department to take the can for some greedy bastard in the MOD who thought back in the eighties Bessomthwaite 288 was an item saleable on the international munitions market." Fenton was indignant. "And may I remind you too, Minister, that it is best I make the decision who in my department gets eliminated."

"Point taken, my dear fellow," the minister said, his tone at once conciliatory and disowning. "I just don't want to be the one that's dragged into number ten after CNN or the Washington Post has the story plastered across the world's media."

"I understand your concerns, Minister, but trust me everything will be done to protect your position. It has always been so has it not?"

"But you don't even know where he is. He could be out there right now," the minister protested in a moment of panic which quickly subsided. "Let me know only if things deteriorate. I'll handle Langley."

"I think we understand one another perfectly, Minister, and thank you for your trust. But with due respect, sir, I believe we have conveniently skated over one of the wider implications of our situation," said Fenton, playfully.

"And which little implication did our skates slither over and slice into two whilst we were doing so?" The minister had caught the hint of Fenton's jocular mood.

"If we were to consider the worse case scenario just on an ethical level for a moment, the quantity of Bessomthwaite 288 he is likely to have, if released in London could wipe out human life in the whole of the capital in a matter of days," Fenton suggested and smiled at the minister as he did so. "Surely our careers and honours matter far less."

"And that is what I like about you, Sir Geoffrey, in the midst of all these horrendous possibilities you have found the humanity, you consider the human cost. You always seem to be able to find the good in any situation."

"Good! Sorry I don't follow you," Fenton looked a little mystified.

"He could be out there right now your man. You fail, he doesn't, is worst case scenario, do you agree?" asked the minister.

"Yes," Fenton replied without reservation.

"Then why the need for worry?" The minister turned and pointed up at the sour-faced portrait of Queen Elizabeth1. "In that event there will only be her left who'll know we fucked-up." They both laughed out loud.

"But still we must do our duty," Fenton remarked.

"Indeed we must still be seen to do our duty," said the minister, almost conceding the point. "Still, enough of this philosophising, how about that drink?"

"I believe we've earned one, but another time perhaps? I'd best get back, you realise," Sir Geoffrey admonished.

"You're right of course," agreed the minister. "Here's to having next times," he added with a hopeful laugh.

"Indeed," Sir Geoffrey said and he left the minister to wonder whether Ms Hoskins would still bed him when he was no longer 'The Minister'.

Chapter Eleven

Enemy at the Gate

"No-one can just disappear," Sir Geoffrey Fenton protested. His tone suggested mild irritation only, not at all the true extent of his desperation.

He had taken a short but slow walk across Westminster Bridge from The House to his department's offices. Through the grey morning's rush hour, seemingly unaware of the pressing throng of humanity streaming past him, he had ambled back towards their drab but imposing old building in Belvedere Road. He had stopped once to peer over the wide parapet of the bridge and ponder on just what he would now be obligated to do but the murky waters of the Thames had offered up no comfort to him. Any way he reviewed his predicament he always arrived at the same and unavoidable conclusion. So he had called his team together on his return and they were sitting there before him now awaiting his instructions.

"Seven days, nothing, and now this," Sir Geoffrey continued. "Where was the last sighting? Has there still been nothing since Weymouth? We have to find him, and quickly." This interim conclusion and his questions were intended for everyone there to digest, so he allowed time for the importance of them to seep into the atmosphere of the room. They all looked tired and dishevelled. They, like he, had not slept since the person to person telephone call from an old friend in the Iraqi Intelligence Service had woken Fenton late the previous evening. Warning of a possible anthrax attack on the capital to be delivered by one of the team's own agents was information which Fenton had needed to treat seriously, so everyone had been mobilised immediately.

The long room where they were gathered was dark despite panels of pale morning daylight oozing in through five tall narrow windows which overlooked the Thames. It's high ceilings had often reverberated to the shouts and echoes of much of our nation's dark and troubled history. On it's oak panelled walls hung large landscapes which depicted great and decisive moments in many, famously victorious, battles. Portraits of long dead generals and air chief marshals glowered down on the small assembly as if to demand even greater deeds of valour from these precious few defenders of the nation. Fenton, standing at the head of the table reigned in his overwhelming feelings of loss and betrayal, drew a breath and continued.

"The new policy of open house does not apply to this situation. I am sure you all understand we need a low profile action on this one. None of the other sections are to be involved unless absolutely necessary. We must clean this up ourselves. He's one of our own and the department is expected to deal with the situation swiftly but more importantly, spotlessly. This most definitely belongs outside the public domain, if the press got hold of this, well, it could start a widespread panic." He paused as if weighing up how best to continue.

"Of course, if the Americans get even so much as a whiff, they'll demand to be involved and that's the last thing we need. One of their agents has already been found dead in Baghdad, with all the hallmarks of Eric's, *special techniques*." Fenton stressed the two words. "Been dead for four days, apparently.

It took them two days to identify the body it was so badly burnt."

He sat down and opened out the blue folder on the table in front of him. It contained a large coloured photograph and a typewritten report, from which he began to read.

"Günter Metzer, German working for the CIA in Baghdad, reporter on the paper Hamburger Zietung. What a mess!" he added, after looking at the picture. He continued, "We have authority from the highest level to act according to needs. Lomas may well be a fully paid-up member of our little club but I am afraid we have to treat this information from Iraq very seriously. General Mahmud Hassan is an honourable but clever man. In allowing Eric to leave Iraq unchallenged he has allowed a situation to develop that could be of great benefit to those within the IIS, and of great benefit to his country at the same time. What a coup it would be for them if we do have a rogue agent on our hands. If this intelligence is genuine, and I'm inclined to believe it is, it seems this could very well be the case. My assessment is that Lomas has re-entered the country in the way he has, specifically to avoid detection and his determination to keep his whereabouts secret from us only reinforces that view. Therefore, irrelevant of the fact he is one of us, Eric Lomas has become a major threat to the security of this country. So it falls to us, we unhappy few, to find him and stop him.

"So where the hell is he now?"

Fenton's unit was never ever mentioned in the running of daily business at the Palace of Westminster and seldom even in the clandestine corridors and rooms of Whitehall, so to all intents and purposes it did not exist. It did not exist in much the same way as S.I.9 of the Special Bureau of the Iraqi Intelligence Service did not exist. Fenton's unit had no official name either, the Defence Intelligence Service being a title attributed to a different section entirely that specialized in fact finding and number crunching. His group, although required sometimes to act upon conclusions drawn from DIS information, remained separate and virtually unnoticed. They used DIS stationery from time to time, and sometimes borrowed a pen or two. It was they alone who referred to themselves as 'The Club' They had been only seven in number including Lomas, their most experienced field operative, until Fenton had temporarily suspended him from operations. DIS personnel however referred to them as the Secret Seven. They were often mentioned in frustration following questions such as:

"Where the hell have all the notepads gone, again?"

"Where the hell do you think? Jan from Secret Seven took an armful yesterday, so they now no longer officially exist."

Four of these notebooks were placed now on the table in front of the three men and one woman who listened to Fenton's words in disbelief.

"Keswick, sir. Err, last sighting that is. A specialist arms unit last evening requested the details on the registration plate we are looking for. The unit, an unmarked Granada with one officer, have been off air since then. It has now, just this morning been designated as missing." It was David Lawson who cut into the nervous quiet that had grown suddenly in the room like Jack's magic beanstalk.

"Keswick!" Fenton blasted back at him. "Keswick?" Fenton repeated, as if questioning the veracity of this new information. "What in God's name is he doing in Keswick, Duffy?"

Lawson had been with the department or rather 'Little Club' as Fenton liked to call it, since its inception and had worked with Fenton before on a couple of operations under the old system. He felt they had developed a degree of respect for one another beyond the boundaries of age and rank that enabled him to speak where the others were more likely to be wary of Sir Geoffrey's legendary and often vocal inability to suffer fools gladly. The old man had used his old nick-name 'Duffy' so Lawson knew he was on fairly safe ground and continued.

"Well, Sir Geoffrey, up to now, eluding us and making a good job of it I would say, wouldn't you Sir?"

"Indeed, but not anymore. We must get…" He was interrupted by an insistent knocking at the door.

"Yes come!" he shouted, annoyed he would lose his train of thought.

The heavy oak double doors parted and a small, smart, handsome young woman entered. It was Fenton's daughter, who was also Fenton's secretary and the seventh member of the unit.

"Yes, Angela, what is it?" his voice once again showing irritation at this interruption.

"So sorry to disturb, but I have an urgent message for Major Lawson." She replied in such a flat, even and unruffled tone it was obvious that she was not sorry and paid scant attention to her father's customary tantrums.

"Go ahead then, girl. Get on with it." Fenton got up from his chair at the head of the table and went to one of the tall, leaded-light windows overlooking the river. As he stood watching the silver Thames thread its way through that grey London morning he contemplated for a moment the seriousness of this breach in security and its undoubted repercussions within the entire secret service if not dealt with quietly and effectively.

Angela Fenton placed a green folder on the table beside David Lawson and leaned forward to whisper something in his ear, allowing her pearls to dangle on his shoulder. He smiled as the subtle scent of her drifted into his nostrils, but gave no reaction or reply to what she had said. She walked slowly from the room as Lawson, with only the briefest of glances in her direction, opened the folder and began to read its contents.

"They've found the car he stole in Weymouth, up there in Cumbria, sir," he announced. "It was hidden in trees on the B5289 which runs along the eastern shore of Derwentwater just south of Keswick. It seems there is a dead policeman in it."

"From the armed response unit?" asked Fenton from the window.

"It appears so, sir, yes."

"And the unit?"

"No trace as yet, sir," Lawson replied.

"Good work, David, good work. Perfect, that has helped us a lot. Now we can really get started," Fenton exhorted. As a reaction to the news of a dead policeman being found, this was not one that for many would immediately have come to mind: but they all knew what he meant. Now there was a manhunt underway for a police killer they could move with greater freedom, slide down between the cracks of an official investigation, and cover-up any of those cracks that could lead their way.

"The rest of you can go, see if you can find out where he's been these past seven days. I need to speak to Major Lawson alone. Colonel Lomas seems to be heading north rather than coming to London for us, so I want comprehensive lists of all sensitive installations in the area around Keswick, places where he could be aiming to do us the most damage. We must assume the Iraq intelligence is correct, and he intends to do this country a great deal of harm. You've got an hour to come up with a list and your best guesses. Major Lawson will come and brief you individually when I've finished with him."

They each stood slowly, pushing their chairs back as they did so and without comment picked up their notepad, which of course did not officially exist and quietly filed out of the room, heads down, dejectedly. Even though he had resumed his watch on the river Fenton detected their rather sullen demeanour and when the thick heavy oak doors had closed soundlessly again he spun round on his heels leaving his contemplations unresolved.

"They seem a bit down in the mouth, Duffy, what's up?"

"I think they're just exhausted, sir." Lawson hesitated before continuing. He knew Sir Geoffrey had not slept the previous night either, but for many different reasons he suspected. Eric Lomas was like a son to Sir Geoffrey, so for him this would be far more traumatic than the rest of The Club could possibly imagine; like having a favourite child turn bad. David Lawson had learned it was better to say little and listen in these situations, so he determined he would wait to be asked for an opinion. After all he had no idea yet what role Sir Geoffrey had in mind for him to play in this unfolding drama: he was however about to find out.

"They have done bloody well, and working in the dark most of the time too. Linking that stolen Fiesta to the times ferries arrived in Weymouth was clever work." Fenton came back to the table and sat down. "I should never have allowed him to go, Duffy."

"Still can't be absolutely sure it's him, sir. There's no real evidence that it is him, only the Iraqi's suggestion." Lawson turned over several of the pages in his opened blue folder and forgetting his most recent resolution to keep his opinions to himself, went further. "This is not Eric. He's the most trustworthy and loyal member of this unit. He wouldn't turn on his own country like this? I mean why would he, especially now Katherine and his boys are gone? He needs his friends more now than ever before. He's probably still in Iraq, undercover, serving Queen and country in his own particularly sinister way."

It was now Sir Geoffrey Fenton's turn to consider momentarily the direction this briefing would take.

"Not too long after the Iraqis released information about the graves at al-Razazah it was you, David, who pointed out to me how his behaviour had changed and was becoming uncharacteristically haphazard and erratic," Sir Geoffrey reminded him.

"I'm sure you had noticed it too, sir."

"Until then I think he had accepted they were gone, but then news from Kabala and the sudden uncertainty as to just how they may have died, I believe began to cloud his judgement: that was why I suspended him. I mean before, would he have stayed out of contact for seven days? He has not used his phone or any of his credit cards even, solely to prevent us finding him. He would always give us some way of tracking him, of letting us know where he was. Before he knew they were definitely killed he would not have behaved this way." Fenton paused.

"Do you like him?" Fenton asked Lawson, suddenly.

"He is my comrade-in-arms, of course."

"No. Would you say he is a friend?"

"Well yes, I'd say he was a friend. I find him rather scary though, some of the stories I've heard. Dangerous to know, but then that's his forte isn't it, that's what he does. I mean that's what makes him as effective as he is, not to mention attractive to women. Yes, I like him. Why? Is that important?"

"Could you kill him if you had to?" asked Fenton, pinning Lawson's astonished gaze with his icy blues. He could see the conflict going on behind Lawson's surprised stare. Fenton brought a hand down slowly on the dark polished expanse of table between them with a soft thump. "You don't have to answer that. I know the answer already. We never know, until that moment. A friend is a friend until he turns into a threat."

Fenton closed his blue folder, opened the red one he had in front of him and scanned the top page of the three it contained, saying nothing. He had read them earlier with minute interest. He turned to the second page beneath the first, again saying nothing even when he'd finished with it and had turned to the last page. He was looking for a conclusion, alternative to the one he had made following his first reading.

"None of this is conclusive. That's why I am sure it is him. He never leaves a trail that anyone else can follow but us. Now even we have managed to lose him for seven days."

"That still doesn't make it him, sir."

"It's him, and he is up to something. Keswick makes it him. Read this and I am sure you will agree." Fenton closed the red folder and handed it to Lawson. Red folder, classified, eyes only. It was rare for Fenton to break with fundamental security practices in this way. Lawson hesitated before opening the folder.

"Read the dammed report, man, don't worry about protocol, if this goes pear-shaped it will all be common knowledge soon enough. Read, that's an order."

"Aye aye, sir."

Fenton got up from the table and drew a decanter of whisky from the tantalus that sat on a robust Jacobean sideboard beside his favourite window. He poured a substantial measure of antique Laphroiag into a cut glass rummer. He took a long sip and waited for the harsh burning liquid to melt into its fragrant peaty, sea-weedy glow. He allowed this first mouthful of the single malt to slip down slowly into his stomach, to feel its warmth spread through him like the fingers of an incoming tide, before turning his attentions to the Thames again. It flowed under the bridges, like a line drawn in silver ink, between the narrow arches, around the wide piles of brick and concrete which supported them, away beyond the misty horizon to the sea. He remembered for a moment why he cherished this view above most others, albeit the memory it now evoked was tinged with a moment of sadness and regret.

Chapter Twelve

Hungarian Memory

As David Lawson read, Sir Geoffrey Fenton allowed himself to be carried back forty years, to different bridges, to a different river; in another city and another country. A lot of water has flowed under those bridges in Budapest since then, he thought.

The waters of the Danube were freezing that night in 1960. A small unit of men, led by Colonel William Lawson, David's father, were given the task of extracting the young, brilliant and beautiful biochemist Ilyana Kadich.

She was twenty-seven and head of her team in pathogenic mutation research when the five blackened faces of her saviours appeared dripping wet at her door, armed with an array of semi-automatic weapons, at the dead of night. One of them asked her quietly and politely if she would like to take a swim. Fenton smiled to himself, remembering the impish twinkle in those eyes when she replied, "You have come all this way, I should be rude if I refuse." English spoken in her Hungarian accent; infectious and fatally attractive.

Born in Budapest in 1933 she was only eleven when Soviet forces had laid siege to the city towards the end of World War Two. Ilyana survived World War Two by a mixture of good luck and guile. She hated the Nazis even before they occupied Hungary in 1944. She was ten years old then, but only eight when the Fascist Government of Hungary convicted her father of treason and had him publicly executed by firing squad in front of the Parliament Buildings. She watched his body jerk this way and that as the bullets slapped into him. She watched him crumple, head hanging forward, still half standing, quite dead but held up still by the ropes they used to bind his legs and arms to the killing post. She watched as the officer in German uniform ordered his squad to shoulder their arms. She watched as the officer marched up to her father's body and drew his Luger from its leather pouch. She watched as he placed the end of the barrel carefully on her father's head and shot two bullets into it. The German officer barked out another order and she watched the soldiers of the firing squad obediently march off. They were all Hungarian. She and her mother pleaded with her two elder brothers not to join the resistance in the heat of revenge. With their father no longer with them, they were needed to protect the family home. Like the good sons they were, both refrained from seeking retribution for the murder of their father.

But in 1944 when the Germans came in force to occupy Budapest and make a stand against the advancing Soviet Armies, they came back with an entirely different army. No longer the arrogant all conquering master race they had been. They were young frightened reinforcements for a crumbling Russian front. They had not come as friends this time, as allies maybe, but not as friends. They were angry.

Many of the soldiers were younger than her brothers. Ilyana and her mother, with all their pleading could not stop them this time. They had endured six months of Nazi occupation and humiliation. They had been patient long enough. They too were angry.

One morning her brothers left very early, before it was light. Their tracks, left in the mid-December snows, led off over the hill towards revenge and patriotism. Ilyana never saw them again. They got lost somewhere in the hundred days of hell that wiped out eighty percent of Budapest. The Russians were at the gates of the city, and they were angry too.

Sir Geoffrey Fenton took another slug from the rummer of whiskey. Duffy was still reading.

She had cried in his arms the night she had told him her story, cried as though she could never stop. She cried like that because she could not cry before. She was in England now, she felt safe. She was twenty-eight, and cried like a baby but with an adult's understanding of what had happened to her as a child. It had crushed him, the thought her spirit, her endurance, her brilliance could so easily have been snuffed out, become lost to the world; like her brothers. He had fallen in love with her then. If he had not known this before he understood it then as she continued, through her tears, to describe the effects of the Nazi and Soviet bombardment of the city.

Axis forces, refusing to surrender, as Hitler had commanded, were pounding the advancing Soviet forces with the same viciousness the Russians were pounding them. Both armies intent on destroying each other managed, gradually, to reduce most of Budapest to rubble. In a continuous barrage from heavy guns and air-raids, for one hundred days bombs and shells dropped in the vicinity of Ilyana's home. Day and night their grand old house was rattled by the closeness of the impacts and there were several direct hits from shelling by the artillery. In the end it became impossible to determine whether they were Russian or German shells and bombs that were falling on their home. In the end it didn't really much matter to Ilyana and her mother, the effect was just the same: utter terror.

As the Ukrainian and Russian armies surrounded the city, the German and Hungarian armies became trapped either side of the river and so too did the civilian population. Ilyana and her mother lived hidden in the basement of their old house in Pest for more than two months. They had managed to store tinned foods that her brothers had liberated before they went missing. For their drinking water, twice a day Ilyana risked collecting fresh snow from the garden at the front of their shattered house in a large tin can. Sometimes she would recover chunks of meat from the snow. Frozen pieces of flesh from the stiff dead horses left lying partially butchered in the street outside, or cut from other animals killed during the bombings, were left kindly there in the garden by one or other of her many starving neighbours for her to find. Each day when she went out she noticed the appearance of more sky and fewer buildings and each day she noticed her mother getting weaker and weaker. Their city was gradually being demolished and its population starved from existence.

Each day there were more bodies of soldiers left where they had fallen like so many toppled statues frozen in death, the winter snow holding off the full horror and stench of their putrefying flesh. Then one morning in February 1945, just before the remaining Germans escaped and the Hungarian army unconditionally surrendered, she was spotted collecting snow in the garden by a soldier. He was wearing a Russian's uniform and carried a long rifle. He followed her into the smashed house. His hot breath blew out clouds into the cold air as he chased her down the steep stairs into their basement. He was covered in mud and grime and he stank. Her mother went to attack him with a garden fork, but he just smashed it aside with his rifle butt and punched her straight in the face. Ilyana, frozen with fear, peed herself as she watched the brute rip at her mother's clothes as she lay half-conscious on the stone floor. He unbuttoned the front of his trousers and sat astride her partially naked body and raped her whilst attempting to bite at her exposed breasts. When he finally finished with her he shot her in the forehead twice with his hand gun.

He was still sitting astride her when a Russian officer appeared, large at the top of the staircase. He must have heard the shots. He was a big man and stood, legs apart with his hands behind his back assessing the scene below him. The brute looked up at him and laughed.

"There's a pretty little one down here for you, Comrade Colonel, especially reserved for officers only."

The Russian officer brought his hand from behind his grey greatcoat and pointed it and the pistol he held in it at the brute's head and fired without a word spoken. The brute fell forward onto Ilyana's mother, still jerking spasmodically. The officer slowly descended the stair into their basement, one step at a time and shot the twitching soldier a second time. This time he placed the barrel of his pistol carefully at the back of the brute's head, where the spine joins the skull.

Fenton remembered he had pointed out, when Ilyana was telling him the story, that she had noted that precision before, and he had explained to her then why it was most effective. He remembered her reaction had been one of fascination rather than revulsion, saying she found it interesting that some can kill with no thought and yet others with such care, with a desire to see it done in the best way possible, like a ritual almost. Ilyana had then just calmly resumed her tale.

The Russian officer unbuttoned the front of his grey greatcoat and sheathed his pistol in its brown canvas pouch. He removed his coat and walked slowly towards Ilyana. He had not yet spoken a single word. He went around behind her and took his coat in both hands and laid its huge warmness over her tiny shoulders. She tried to scream but no sound would come. He faced her, and kneeling down wrapped his arms around her and kissed her forehead.

"Do not be afraid, little one, I will not assault you. I am sorry I have only a few words in your language. Assault is not right word, harm is better I think. I will not harm you." His voice was deep and strong and heavy with Russian, but it was a soft and comforting voice. Ilyana's desire to scream faded before she had even made a peep.

"You must come with me now to my headquarters, it is too dangerful for you here on your own. They can take good care of you here and I will send some mans to bury this womans."

Ilyana pulled away from him and went to her mother. She tried to get the brute off her but he was too heavy. The Russian came and pushed him with his boot so the brute would flop over onto his back on the stone floor. She went to her mother to cover her privacy as best she could.

"She is your mooda I think, yes?"

"Da," Ilyana replied.

"You have a little Russian too I see. That's good. I have men just outside, they will bring your mooda too for proper goodbye. We see to her, Da?"

"Da!" Ilyana stood up and with all the fierceness and malice her young heart could muster spat on the brute and said a very bad word, which the Russian would not understand.

"We Russians are not like him. He is Ukrainian, and he is pig, a common and uneducated human being," said the Russian seriously, attempting to reassure her.

Ilyana gathered up the masses of coat that dragged behind her and ascended the steps. She looked back down the steps into the basement as the Russian officer was covering her mother's body with the Ukrainian's coat. The body of the brute lay there exposed, spread-eagled on the stone floor, his spent lifeless cock lolling limply from the front of his trousers. She watched the Russian officer take hold of the hands of the soldier and placed them over it and she said, in perfect Russian,

"I haven't seen one before. I must admit I was expecting something a little larger."

The Russian officer laughed but gave her a most reprimanding look.

"A Ukrainian, I mean," she explained, again in Russian.

They both laughed loudly.

"I see I'm going to have good trouble with you, young lady," he said through his laughter. He bounded up the steps and followed Ilyana out into the freezing daylight. He stood in front of her, came to attention and saluted her.

"I am Colonel Nicolai Arshavin at your service. These are my men, good Russians each and every one. If anyone of them offends you, they will answer to me. Is that understood, comrades?"

"Da, Comrade Colonel," replied eight loud Russian voices.

"And if anyone else offends you," he looked into her sweet face, "they will have to answer to them, yes?" and opened his hand towards his men.

"Da, Comrade Colonel," they all replied, as one.

"My name is Ilyana Kadich of Pest, may I welcome you to my city, what is left of it."

"As you see, comrades, she speaks good Russian, so take care with your filthy mouths too."

"Da, Comrade Colonel."

"We must go. Four of you to the basement," he ordered. "Two bring the womans, two bury the Ukrainian pig, face down somewhere and return to headquarters. Come we go." He picked Ilyana up in his arms and carried her off to a new life.

In 1957 Dr Philip Lomas, Britain's top biochemist lobbied the government and the opposition to bring dissident physicists and bio-chemists to England from behind the Iron Curtain. As he was then heading the newly reincarnated biological and chemical weapons project his voice was listened to. He felt if these bright minds were willing to be rescued from the Soviet's oppressive regime it would be better to have them working on their specialised projects in Britain rather than elsewhere. He had met with several of these men and women at various international conferences and had gained the respect and trust of many of them.

There was one young woman in particular, Ilyana Kadich, whom he admired not for her quick mind alone, she was also very beautiful. He had assumed, incorrectly, she was Russian as she had studied at the Moscow State University and spoke fluent Russian. He was surprised to learn however, she was an orphan who had been adopted in Budapest at the end of the war by a Russian army colonel, who lavished her with the warmth and love and comfort she had lost. The best schools and opportunities the State could provide were not enough for his Ilyana. She told Dr Lomas after one seminar they both attended, she had returned to Budapest following Nicolai Arshavin's death to do more research in the field of immunology and found herself now working for the State bio-chemical weapons programme. Here was an ideal candidate

142

for his own programme to present to the ministers in Whitehall, Dr Lomas had thought.

Finally realising the benefits of having these people on their side and not in the pockets of the communists, the government agreed to set up a task force and Colonel William Lawson was instructed to devise a plan to bring to Britain any dissident eastern European scientist who expressed a desire to flee the evil clutches of their communist state.

William Lawson and Geoffrey Fenton had worked together before in North Africa during the battle of El Alamein and the recapture of Tobruk where, under the tutelage of David Sterling they formed the nucleus of an embryonic SAS and between them created havoc and mayhem amongst Rommel's retreating forces and the Axis armies as they were chased up through Sicily and Italy in 1944. A seasoned, battle-hardened professional soldier by then, Fenton was still not quite nineteen. Fenton had been so effective as his wartime operations man that Lawson had no hesitation asking Fenton to join him again in 1956 to draw up invasion plans during the Suez crisis, which were never used. Lawson and Fenton were also required at that time to consider a possible military response to the occupation of Hungary by the Russian army following the uprising that same year. So it was that Fenton got the nod in 1958 to put together a small task force of highly trained special services personnel for the purpose of extractions from sensitive or hostile areas in Eastern Europe.

Using the code name Operation Gazelle, an obtuse reference to fence jumpers no doubt, the team G Force, as they nicknamed themselves had by 1960 already completed several successful missions, and had managed to extract eleven eminent scientists from various Warsaw Pact countries. These were completed successfully mainly by eliciting assistance from local groups prepared to smuggle dissidents to the West.

The plan for the Budapest extraction had been his own Fenton recalled, but the operation differed from the other missions in that this was a single extraction and of a female who would only deal directly with one man whom she had met several times at her university in the early fifties before the uprising, and before the Russian tanks had rolled in. Dr Philip Lomas, whom he had never met, was the only person she would trust. Although it was her case that had persuaded the government to act in the very beginning, it had taken Dr Lomas two years to encourage her to leave her home. He had to be there on the day otherwise she would not come out. A civilian on the team meant one less specialist. That was not ideal. The fact that the whole area was in the tight grip of an army of occupation also promised to make things a little more exciting, and necessitated a more secretive and possibly aggressive approach.

Under cover of darkness on a moonless night there had been no problems getting to the house. Dr Lomas too had responded well to the two days intensive training he received at the hands of the Harris brothers, and Fenton had found him an agile and keen participant in this most unusual adventure. An armed Russian foot patrol was spotted early near the western end of one of the bridges so the five man squad, led by Colonel William Lawson, slipped silently down the west bank of the Danube and into the river north of the city. Each holding his sten gun high out of the water, allowing the current to take them noiselessly downstream towards the south western district of the city, they passed unnoticed under the reconstructed bridges, leaving the Russian patrols above blissfully unaware that anything other than driftwood had floated by.

They moved up through the old town of Buda. Very few of the old buildings remained, most were new and shiny. Reconstruction of the city was nearly completed. At the corner of an old building a dark doorway showed a greenish light. It was the only light at two in the morning. They had arrived.

Dr Lomas rubbed some blacking onto Ilyana's lovely face as she gabbled away to him in whispered incomprehensible Hungarian. They seemed like old friends. She was dressed in the dark clothes she had been instructed to wear. She put on a dark woollen hat and the team became six. Colonel Lawson opened the door onto the street and listened.

"Go, I'll cover," he whispered.

Moving cautiously through the unlit Buda streets, folding themselves into every available shadow they made their way back to the river. Fenton roped Ilyana to him as they slid again into the cold waters of the Danube, allowing its current to carry them downstream again, south, under one last bridge and they were out of the city. Ten minutes later and they were scrambling up the muddy bank where two small rubber boats had been carefully hidden the day before. Fenton draped a large thick blanket around Ilyana and rubbed her shivering limbs vigorously to warm and dry her a little. Through chattering teeth she thanked him.

With three to each boat they prepared to push off from the shore. Ilyana, Fenton and Dr Lomas in the first boat got away. Using a short oar each, the two men pulled away quickly and silently from the bank. Fenton could just glimpse in the shadows, over Ilyana's shoulder, Colonel Lawson standing, back to the water covering Nobby Harris and his brother, Archie, ready to embark, stepping into the boat before they merged with the enveloping darkness. Fenton gave Ilyana his oar and made an attempt to get the small outboard started, judging they would soon be far enough away from the shore for the noise it made to go unnoticed from the opposite shore. The engine didn't fire. He tried it again and again it didn't start. Suddenly the darkness from whence they came was rent with the bright explosions of grenades and heavy machine gun fire.

In the flashes Fenton and his companions could see Colonel Lawson standing in the shallow water by the bank, sten gun blazing away. The Harris brothers in the dinghy were also firing when their boat received a direct hit from a grenade. It and they were immediately distributed in very small pieces along the margins of the river. Fenton tried the motor again, it coughed this time but died.

Looking back Fenton could just make out the fallen shape of his old friend and wartime comrade Willie Lawson bent over, face in the mud surrounded by grey greatcoats of the Russian soldiers. He heard two shots from a hand gun. The body slumped forward and moved no more. Then bullets started to hiss and spit closer to their boat. The other two were rowing furiously now and were making good headway. He primed the small outboard once more and this time pulled the lanyard so hard and fast that when the engine caught the lanyard came away in his hand. But the outboard had fired into life this time and, amid the crackle of machine gun fire that popped and fizzed in the water all around their boat, they sped away.

Following through with his plan, Fenton found the old barge and its Austrian captain waiting further downstream as arranged. The Russian soldiers would concentrate their efforts, he hoped, searching for them along the west bank, south of

Buda and not expect them to head for Austria in the opposite direction or from the Pest shore. The old barge was just one of the many coal barges that still plied a trade along the Danube, as they had done for centuries. The three of them lay hidden in its hold under a thin layer of dusty coal sacks. The old barge chugged slowly northwards back through the city along the east bank of the river, hardly making a getaway at all. Among the other barges moving along the river that night, Fenton and Dr Philip Lomas with one extra companion this time, passed once more under the bridges of Budapest, and were again unnoticed. Well away from the searching lights of the troops, they encountered no further hostile attention. At the border their captain had joked with the Russian soldiers; they knew him. He was okay. They checked his manifest, they lifted a tarpaulin or two, without much enthusiasm, and they smoked his western cigarettes. He made a joke of something and laughed with them. He was okay, they let him through.

So his plan had worked and they made good their escape to Vienna and back to the west. *But at no small cost*, Fenton thought.

Colonel William Lawson was awarded, posthumously, a high class medal for bravery under fire, not for laying down his life that night though, but as a retrospective gesture for a raid he had made against heavy odds at Sidi Birani in 1943. There were no official acknowledgements of the events of that night, from either the Soviet authorities or British Intelligence. Although it was generally felt that these events had more than a little to do with the building of the Berlin Wall less than a year later, it was deemed more appropriate to draw a veil over the whole embarrassing affair than to have a full government enquiry; a decision much easier to take in those days. G Force was subsequently disbanded, the general feeling in British

Army Intelligence being that to go for the thirteenth boffin was perhaps a bridge too far. And so the whole episode was quickly and quietly swept under the carpet of daring do; and forgotten.

Fenton had not forgotten though, and neither had he forgotten the loss of his great friend and mentor. He turned his attention away from the Thames and his memories, back to the work of the day. David Lawson had closed the red file shut, having read each page twice and was now sitting there in stunned silence.

Chapter Thirteen

Sir Geoffrey's Confession

"What are your thoughts on what you've just read?" Draining his glass Fenton returned to the table and sat down beside Lawson, his mind still some distance away.

While Lawson struggled to formulate an adequate answer Sir Geoffrey looked straight at him for a long moment. Knowing what he was about to ask him to do for his country Fenton wondered whether he should be taking such a chance with him. Having David Lawson on the team had helped Fenton reconcile himself to the loss of a very dear old friend that dark night in Budapest and Lawson had proven many times to be every bit his father's son. He would do his duty, Fenton was sure of that, but David Lawson lacked the cold killer instinct of which his father and Eric Lomas, and even Fenton himself, had more than enough. Maybe this was the single element which made David a far better agent than the lot of them. Fenton knew he could rely on him. He could hardly go into the field himself, he was too rusty now and Eric too quick. It's all up to you now young man, he thought, still looking into Lawson's puzzled face.

"Are you okay, sir?" Lawson asked. He had become aware of Fenton's somewhat preoccupied attention and felt he needed to give himself more time to consider an appropriate answer.

"Yes, Duffy, I am fine. I was just thinking about your father. It's a shame you never knew him. A great man, great man."

"He was killed before I was born, sir. Though mother spoke about him all the time and I've seen photographs of him in different uniforms, very smart in some but in various forms of battledress in others, which I thought were rather scruffy when I was young, but considering the sort of stuff he did I suppose I can forgive him that. You can never really know a person just from pictures, can you? Even so I am very proud of him, you know, and to be his son." Lawson blurted all this out in one long stream of semi-rehearsed phrases, his earlier promise of reticence forgotten like a New Year's resolution by Burn's Night.

"I was with the team he was leading when he was killed."

"Yes, I know. How did he die, sir?"

"I can tell you what he was like, if you wish, but you know I can't answer that question, so I shan't; for your own good you understand."

"I do. It makes us psychologically less effective in what we have to do if we know any specifics of the demise of a close relation or colleague killed in action. Number seven in the Club rulebook I believe," said Lawson mockingly, then quickly added, "No, you are right, sir and I'm okay with the idea I already have of him. I've built a picture of him in my mind which I live with and I should leave that as it is."

"Precisely so, it is advised policy, as you see from the report." Fenton pointed to the red folder on the table.

The three paged closely typed report Lawson studied was in three sections, only two had headings: Assessment of General Mahmud Hassan al Majid's Disclosures and Their Motives, and Mr Eric Lomas SO; Current Psychological

Profile. The section without a heading was an evaluation of the probable outcome, should Lomas discover how his family actually died.

"Is that why Eric wasn't told about the specific nature of the deaths of Katherine and his boys?"

"Again precisely so," Fenton replied. "As you've just read they are concerned now downstairs that Eric, having found an amount of this Bessomthwaite 288 pathogen, has put two and two together, added in the facts surrounding his mother's death and come up with rule number one in his personal Club rulebook: Destroy all traces of that which offends thee."

"Which would seem to imply, sir, he knows precisely how his mother died then," Lawson retorted.

"Indeed, he does. He has known since he was fifteen, long before the directive to restrict such information came into effect. Even so it would have been impossible to keep the details from him in any event, given the circumstances."

Fenton took a breath and continued, "She kept a diary, do you see, which he and I have seen? They were about to test a new strain of anthrax serum using a small monkey. Ilyana was holding the monkey as still as possible, but the monkey squirmed at the vital moment and Dr Philip Lomas injected his wife, Ilyana, with the experimental serum instead of the monkey. They had never had a human subject on whom to test their research before and it was agreed they should attempt to turn what was initially an accident, into an opportunity to study the effects this latest serum would have on a human's immune system and then study also how our immune system affected changes in the pathogen itself.

"Following the initial accident she was expected to make a full recovery of course, after treatment with strong antibiotic. So Ilyana insisted that she should write down every change in her physically and in the make-up of her blood and Philip would look for signs of change in the behaviour of the pathogen. She had anticipated some form of mutation following contact with her blood and its antigens, not realising the catastrophic effect it was having throughout her entire body. She did not recover. Instead she slowly became very ill and died two weeks later. Right up until the last few days she religiously recorded the appearance of any new lesions on her skin and watched, through her microscope, the bugs grow and mutate on slides containing droplets of her contaminated blood. As she became weaker, following massive blood loss through the pores of her skin and eventually when the pain that no amount of morphine could alleviate became too much for her, she had to stop. The last thing she wrote in her last notebook, if I can remember, reads something like," and he began to recite slowly and with apparent difficulty a passage he had obviously memorised word for word.

"'Today my blood has changed colour and texture, it's more like the grounds left in the bottom of a coffee cup. It is as if my blood has suddenly got very old, thick and brown and granular. Like old oil in an unloved car, turned gelatinous and opaque from neglect. It is no longer nourishing, not bright and red and clear as blood should be, not viscous and wholesome, but dark and stiff and toxic; lifeless dead blood. I can no longer continue this I am now too weak, but Philip is here with me. He will carry me on until the end and make this accident mean something. I have made him promise.'

"That's where Eric's single minded dedication stems from. His mother, not me." Sir Geoffrey fell silent and David Lawson could tell well enough this was not a time to steer the briefing back to their more immediate problem.

"So Philip Lomas took over documenting and analyzing the slow, remorseless progress of the serum as his wife's body finally broke down," said Sir Geoffrey, stopping again and then continuing. "After her death every drop of her blood that could be gathered was vacuumed up into sealed storage containers to prevent contamination, which also allowed for a large amount of the pathogen to be stored for closer examination and future development. It was fortunate Lomas and his technicians had been wearing protective clothing as further research on the serum taken from her blood showed that the pathogen had mutated to a point where it was able to survive in air. Outside the body it remains toxic and contagious for over three weeks. It was decided soon after that what was left of her should be incinerated, there in the laboratory." Fenton paused again for a moment, hauling in his emotions. "There was a funeral, Eric attended, but nothing of his mother was buried that day. The risk of contamination was too great, do you see? It was a grim business."

"You were very close to her, sir?" Lawson risked asking.

"Close, yes. We were lovers, Duffy, soul mates they say these days, don't they? But she wanted to marry and she felt a great sense of loyalty to Philip. It was he who had rescued her from a life of tyranny in 1960s Hungary after the Russians swept in. And me, I was too loyal to the service to expect her to give up her work and become my wife. It was that which drove her, her work made her who she was. With Philip she could have both a husband and her work, I would only have taken that from her, and sometimes I wish I had. Perhaps she would still be alive if I had. A month later she and Philip were married, with young Eric on the way. They were happy, but if I hadn't rejected her maybe she would still be here. They would both still be here. My grandchildren would still be here.

But I was still on active service then, do you see? I felt marriage at the time would have been too much of a tie. It remains a decision of which I am still not especially proud, Duffy."

"You shouldn't think like that, Sir Geoffrey. She would still have wanted to do her work, wouldn't she?"

"You don't understand. If we had married, as she asked, I could be playing happily with our grandchildren now. Instead she is dead and I, I have become Abraham." His words faded to a whisper.

"What did you say, sir?" Lawson enquired innocently.

"I have become like Abraham. Prepared to slaughter his only son for his God, my God being this department and the system which sanctions its actions." There was a sudden bitter edge to his voice.

"Are you saying that he...?" Lawson didn't finish the question.

"Ye, Duffy, Eric is my son. I am Eric Lomas's biological father and to serve the God I have chosen I have to send you to kill him, before he wipes out half the population of Northern England." He stood up and walked to the window again.

"I understand the situation is still very serious but isn't that a bit extreme, sir? Is there no other way? Surely when we find him he can be immobilized, some form of stun weapon, I don't know. Then bring him back in for rehab or something like that." Lawson knew he was clutching at straws. "God did spare Isaac didn't he?"

"Yes, so he did. And don't think I haven't considered all the alternatives? There would be other options if this Bessomthwaite 288 were not so toxic. We, Abraham's children have become destroyers of nations. I fear we may have finally broken our covenant with God and our only

154

chance now is a professional hit before Eric can release His vengeance."

"Does Angela know he is her half-brother? I mean she was very close to him growing up, with him living in your house and everything. When we were teenagers I thought she only had eyes for him. Then something happened and she suddenly loathed him." Lawson felt a little uneasy speaking about Angela. He wasn't sure Sir Geoffrey would approve of their developing relationship.

"You and Margret, my late wife, are the only persons who know he is really my son; and Eric of course. Even Philip Lomas didn't know until after Ilyana died. I didn't know until after she died either, although I had long suspected the truth. He came to see me, Philip, not long after Ilyana's funeral and he confronted me with it. He had found some references to our affair written in one of her private diaries. She had always believed the baby to be mine and never told me. She married Philip Lomas as some sort of revenge I suppose; a bit like Angela's interest in you, dear boy. That started out as a way to hurt Eric for his rejection of her."

Lawson shifted uneasily in his chair. He was acutely aware that any serious relationship existing within the service was seen to compromise national security.

"Did you think I hadn't noticed?"

David Lawson remained silent and inscrutable, but he felt a sudden flush spreading below his collar.

"Don't bother yourself about it, boy, I am pleased for you both. We must all find a little happiness where and when we can. It isn't as if she is likely to be operational. Can get a little messy though, personal relationships out in the field."

Fenton continued, "Yes, anyway she pursued Eric from a very young age. When Eric first came to live with us, Angela followed him everywhere. Margret knew Eric was my son but we thought it cute at first that Angela had taken to him with such enthusiasm. When Eric was seventeen, he'd been with us two years by then, Margret and I had a word with him and persuaded him to avoid giving Angela any encouragement, as he was far too old for her. But as Angela developed into a young woman it became obvious to me that I had to tell Eric the truth. So on his twenty-first birthday, I told him."

"How did he react?"

"He met Katherine soon after. They married and I don't think Angela has ever really forgiven him. Then Katherine had the boys, my grandsons, who are gone now too as you know." Sir Geoffrey thought about having another whisky, but did not.

"I see why downstairs are concerned. They assess his reaction as a kind of waking catatonia by the sound of it, complete breakdown but still able to function on most levels." Lawson opened the red folder to the third page. He read from it.

"'It is more than probable Lomas will utilise all his talents to inflict some form of damage on us, by no means the least of which would be to make it public knowledge that the Ministry of Defence may have been instrumental in providing Saddam with this bio-weapon. Mahmud Hassan has been very shrewd here. He is attempting to use one of our own agents against us.'"

"How did the Iraqis get hold of such a destructive weapon in the first place?" Lawson asked.

"We sold it to them. After the Shah was forced into exile, western governments with concerns over the manner in which Iran was descending into fundamentalism gave Iraq and Saddam's Ba'athist party any assistance it requested to wage a war against Iran, including weaponry. We were of course no exception, but I wish I had been at the meeting which decided to release this particular demon from its box. I was never convinced the Iraqis wouldn't one day turn the weapons we sold them on us. And now they have."

"How so now?" asked Lawson.

Rage welled up in Fenton's voice, virtually spitting out the words. But his anger and frustration was not directed towards Lawson, more at the apparent stupidity of the whole affair.

"Page one, bloody page one, man." Fenton fumed. "You've read it. Just Hassan telling us Eric has brought some of it back here is how, let alone it being brought here by one of our own people and from the very country we sold it to, that's how. Bessomthwaite 288 has come back to bite us in the backside. General Hassan knows we have to react to keep even the existence of Bessomthwaite 288 suppressed. We will probably have to eliminate one of our top agents and then the icing on the cake would come if any of this stuff gets released in London or any major city. Hassan would see that as merely a bonus. It will become an undeniable disaster for which Iraq is bound to take the credit, and all our dirty laundry will be out in public view. Using this Bessomthwaite 288 he is drawing us into war we don't want. We will have to go into Iraq with the Americans when they go after Saddam."

"But why is, just General Hassan telling us, enough on its own?"

"He has been of help to us in the past. There is no doubt in my mind that his intelligence is genuine, though I suspect he set up this whole strategy for his own ends. I had a meeting with the minister earlier today and he assures me the Americans are determined to get Saddam out. They are looking for any excuse to get in there, UN resolutions or no. We however, and I include the prime minister in this, have always wanted to avoid a full scale war in Iraq so we have insisted on a legitimate reason to go in; principally a UN resolution. This can only be achieved it seems by showing that Saddam still has weapons of mass destruction. WMDs is the latest buzz-phrase in Whitehall."

"But they must know he has this stuff, we sold it to him," Lawson persisted.

"Not necessarily. In any event it may be something the government would prefer remained undisclosed, for obvious reasons. But as the inspectors failed to find any WMDs on Iraqi soil, when they were there, Saddam can continue to deny having any and until now we could deny Bessomthwaite 288 ever existed."

Fenton added, "Our government's position has been to wait and allow the UN's sanctions and the resultant dissidence fomenting within Iraq to really take hold, then to support the people who will rise up against Saddam's regime. The Americans aren't as patient as us. It still rankles with the top brass that George senior didn't finish the job when they had him on the run."

"So Mahmud Hassan is giving us proof positive that Iraq has WMDs, knowing we have to react," Lawson said.

"American intelligence is unsure just how much of such types of material with which the West supplied Saddam he actually used during his war with Iran. If they suspected he still has even an insignificant amount of such material left to launch with his scuds into Israel and Saudi Arabia the Americans would need to respond. Proof like this, that Iraq has any amount of weapons of mass destruction hidden, is the undeniable and legitimate reason for going in and getting him out they've been waiting for." Fenton concluded. "And in the face of such compelling evidence, as the possible destruction of a whole swathe of England and its population, it will be hard for the prime minister to resist joining the American crusade regardless of any legal impediment."

"So even if we are able to stop Eric releasing this pathogen, the country will still be compelled to go in with the Americans." Lawson's penny was starting to drop.

"Yes, for the simple reason that the government will have run out of excuses not to. And whatever the security and strategic reasoning behind it, the public will be unforgiving and the government could fall. It is that serious a dilemma. The prime minister will know that theoretically we could legitimately invade Iraq with the Americans, but can't get a resolution passed at the UN to do so without owning up to Bessomthwaite 288."

"The Americans won't worry that it is our stuff that was found, just where it was found," Lawson interjected.

"In a nutshell, dear boy," agreed Fenton. "We are being pushed, by General Hassan and the Americans, into a war without a UN resolution but in the certain knowledge that weapons of mass destruction do exist in Iraq and yet are unable to go public with the proof. The government does not want to go to war. Latest intelligence shows Saddam has destroyed or decommissioned ninety percent of his capability over the last year and the PM has suggested Saddam no longer presents any real threat. Our parliament certainly would not want to go to war following a situation where WMDs, made in Britain were found on Iraqi soil, and they certainly do not want a war that has no UN authorization. The Americans however, will still expect us to join forces with them if they decided to go ahead unilaterally and drag us into an illegal war without UN backing if necessary. It could mean political suicide for the PM, who sanctions it, and probably the end for the current British government. Without this intelligence we can at least refuse Washington on ethical grounds by insisting it would be contradictory to international law to go to war without any definite proof that WMDs still exist. We have had that moral high ground cut away from under our feet so to speak, and if this stuff gets out into the environment the government are sunk any way you look at it. And that is where we come in."

"Yes I see, sir, we have no choice either," Lawson concurred. "General Hassan has been a wiley old fox. But why doesn't he just tell the Americans the situation?"

"He won't need to if Eric releases any here. He hopes they will find out through us. The genie will be out of the bottle by then, so to speak," Fenton suggested. "General Hassan is hoping this will create a split in any new coalition building against his country."

"How much of this stuff does Saddam have?" Lawson asked.

"Not enough to deter the current administration on Capitol Hill unfortunately, only the cache Eric stumbled on in al-Razazah I suspect and that has probably been destroyed by now as per UN requirements, or moved somewhere impossible to trace. If this gets into the media, albeit as common knowledge or as a result of thousands of deaths in Cumbria, the government are sunk or we will be at war within a year, you mark my words."

"What is our next step then, sir?" Lawson knew Sir Geoffrey had taken him into his confidence by sharing all this personal and politically sensitive information. He was determined to reward this trust.

"I want you up there, Duffy, today. See if you can second guess his next move. I'll get on to Special Branch. We don't want the local force getting too enthusiastic.

"Nor Special Branch for that matter, sir," Lawson added.

"Indeed! This could get very messy if not handled correctly," Fenton agreed. "That's why I want you on the scene as it were. You understand now what has to be done. I want swift decisive action. None of this 'talk 'em out of it' palaver that's popular these days. You are not a negotiator, take him out. It gives me great pain to order you to do this and in this way, but in doing so I take full responsibility for the action and its consequences. Those vials must remain intact. Get Angela to pull all the relevant files. I don't care how deep you have to dig, find us something we can work on. There's a dark flight from RAF Henlow this afternoon, you are on it. Any red tape comes up, refer them directly to me and I'll sort it. Okay?"

"Aye-aye, sir!" responded Lawson, emphatically.

Chapter Fourteen

Dark Flight

Later that morning, Major David Lawson sat alone at one of the many unoccupied tables in a rather mediocre roadside diner, with only a large cup of rather mediocre coffee for company. He had driven up from town alone. Sir Geoffrey had arranged for him to join a dark flight as an invisible passenger from RAF Henlow, which was just a few miles further on, off the A1 in Bedfordshire. Angela was to meet him at the diner with the last two top secret files he had wanted to read before leaving London, but she was late. He had intended to read them before he boarded the short flight up to Cumbria. The flight left for RAF Kingstown at noon and Lawson had to be on it, with or without the files. He looked at his watch again. It wasn't quite eleven but he was getting a little anxious nonetheless.

He read from a photocopy of the first page of a report he had hurriedly drawn from the top file on Angela's desk and stuffed into the inside pocket of his jacket before leaving London. The few paragraphs on the page contained a brief synopsis of the workings of a human's immune system. Lawson thought it would give him some insight into the catastrophic effects of Bessomthwaite 288 exposure. He read:

'Human beings are a battlefield. Daily, each one of us comes under attack from infection and disease. It is nothing less than an attempted invasion. Alien organisms try continually to find an entry into the temple of our bodies, with no other intention than the seemingly benign desire to survive themselves and reproduce. They are legion, these forces ranged against us, and their methods of attack and entry are as varied as they are themselves diverse. Bacteria in our food, germs in the air we breathe, bugs in the water we drink, micro-organisms small enough to penetrate our skin, viruses that enter the blood-stream through a wound, these are all regiments in an army of invasion.

Subjected as we are to the massive scale of this onslaught it is a wonder we survive at all, and we would not but for our own army of defence, our inherited defence shield, the immune system. Refined over thousands and thousands of years, our individual immune response can cope with just about all that is thrown at it, but not all.

How it works is highly complex and very fragile.

When the body detects the incursion of a foreign body, i.e. an alien micro-organism, or pathogen, immediately healthy cells, via the blood, flood the area where the invading organism has already begun to multiply and multiply and multiply. Our army of anti-insurgence, the defence cells, known as antibodies, attach themselves to the alien cells as they develop. In a healthy body with a healthy immune system the antibodies will eventually kill off the first wave of occupation.

When the battle is at its height, information on the assailants is gathered by receptor cells and passed back along the line to headquarters: our hypothalamus. This gland, situated at the front of our brains, can then replicate the exact type of antigen necessary to effectively kill off the main force of that particular invading pathogen. Millions upon millions of these specially designed antigens, our immune response, are dispatched like cavalry into the battle to overwhelm and exterminate the remaining hostile pathogens.

Friend and foe fall together until eventually the insurgents are defeated. The dead and dying from both sides are carried away from the action, via the blood, dispersed through the lymphatic system to the kidneys and bowel, and then excreted.

Furthermore, and this is the really clever part, the hypothalamus having done all the initial work replicating its bespoke antigens, stores this acquired intelligence about the enemy in the form of a small number of starter cells for use against any further similar infections. This is the knowledge which prompted the discovery of immunisation.

Clever don't you think? We are amazing creatures but the pathogens are a wily and mutating enemy that learn new ways to penetrate our defensive shield. Every year new vaccines are developed to counteract these new assailants, and by administering the new designer antibodies to trigger our immune response we can more quickly overwhelm the new viruses and bacteria we encounter.

However, all a foreign body would need to do to invade us would be to disguise itself as a friend; appear as something that is already known to us, or be unrecognisable as an enemy. Seen to present no threat to us, there would be no immune response to challenge this enemy. Our defence shield down, we would soon become overwhelmed. It is this which makes Bessomthwaite 288 as effective a bio-weapon as it is. The human immune system does not recognise it as a foreign body so does not initiate our automatic immune response.'

This simplified summary of such a complex organically evolved defence system, Lawson thought, was not unnecessarily naive and patronising. They were in fact some of the most chilling words he had ever read. They described how easily our existence on the planet could be removed. The whole tone of this précis, taken mostly from high school text books, was a striking contrast to its content and so highlighted with greater impact just how far evil men were prepared to go to protect themselves; by destroying themselves and everyone else in the process. These weapons were not intended for defence he concluded, they were intended as retaliation.

Is that what Eric Lomas too had concluded? Is that too what Eric Lomas had in his mind. Retaliation? Lawson hoped not, but understanding what had happened to first his mother and then his father and more recently the announcement about his wife and children, who could blame him? Lawson reached inside his jacket for his weapon, to check it. The thin cloth holster under his right armpit was empty and an iota of panic flushed through him. He had forgotten for a moment where he was, recovering his composure quickly he smiled at this subconscious reflex. The Sig Sauer nine millimetre pistol and silencer he always used, like all Company weaponry in transport, was safely stored away in the locked steel safe welded into the boot of his car as required by health and safety. All the Company's cars were fitted with these metallic arsenals and his dark blue VW Passat was no exception. They were to be used at all times whilst moving weapons around the UK, much to Lawson's dissatisfaction. He considered the inevitable possibility of coming face to face with Lomas and having just a biro in his pocket to be a more serious breach of his own health and safety regulations. Still, it was the significance of his initial involuntary response on finding his holster empty that disturbed him. He realised in that moment he was not relishing at all the prospect of confronting Lomas professionally, with whatever he would have at his disposal.

Eric was a cold fish. Killing had become a sacred art to him, like a ritual, a serious and exact science. Lawson knew Angela Fenton had once held out hopes that she might become Eric's girl, but from Sir Geoffrey's account gathered Lomas had rightly refused her advances after being told she was his step-sister. He imagined Lomas had treated her cruelly from then on and she would have had no idea why. Then Angela and Lawson became an item and she seemed to have relinquished any claims she may have had on his affections. Eric was aware pretty quickly of their developing relationship and pulled Lawson aside one day and explained how painful and sudden Lawson's death would be if he were ever to harm Angela. David remembered his voice being calm and quiet, yet so chilling and filled with menace that Lawson had no reason to doubt the truth or the intent in Eric's words of brotherly affection. Lawson made to go to his jacket again, but stopped himself this time.

"You look a bit jumpy, are you all right?" Angela sat down across the table from him.

"And you are late." He checked his watch. "My flight is at noon. Did you bring the files I asked for?"

She removed two red files from the attaché case she carried and placed them on the table in front of him.

"Yes I am fine, thank you for asking. What do you have to do to get a coffee in this place?" She was far from pleased at having to drive so far from London; their meetings were normally closer to home. "If you were expecting sex this weekend, you should not have dragged me all the way up here, or is this for Queen and Country?"

"Queen and Country I'm afraid."

"Damn, I was afraid you were going to say that," she complained, but smiled as she got up from the table. "I must get a coffee. I guess it is self-service here. You want another?" He was already reading the first of the two files she had brought so he just nodded his assent and she kissed him on top of his head as she passed him. She loved him even more when he got all serious like this.

He was still reading from the first red file when she returned with two cups of steaming coffee. Lawson reached into the inside of his jacket and withdrew the folded photocopy he had been reading earlier and placed it on the table for Angela to read.

"Take a little look at that, and you'll see what I am up against." He hoped it would allow him enough time to finish reading before she started asking more questions. He sipped his coffee and picked up the second red file; both coffee and file were as unpleasant as their predecessors. He had already trolled through a long and uninspiring list of potentially sensitive military installations in the Cumbrian area hoping he might divine from it an obvious target at which Eric might wish to strike. Only one stuck out and was so obvious he was sure Lomas would dismiss it as quickly as he had done.

Lawson was now reading through an account of the tragic circumstances which had brought about the gruesome death of Eric's mother. As if following what he had just read, Angela said quietly, "Imagine dying like that and keeping notes about it at the same time."

"Have you read this?" Lawson enquired.

"Yeh, of course. I had to check they were the right files didn't I? Besides I was held up at dispersal, they didn't have a car ready for me, did they? That's why I was late." Angela sipped at her coffee. "And we developed this here, in this country, did we?" she said, and turned the photocopy face down on the table between them.

"Yes, we did, but I think they were looking for an antidote at the time rather than attempting to enhance its potency. But they don't work on it anymore. Something else was found to be more effective than what the Russians had and research was scrapped twenty years ago. What we had stock-piled, some bright spark in the MOD sold to Saddam to wipe out the Iranians for us."

"Then we are no better than any of the other nutters that are loose in the world. There's a chance too that Eric's wife and kids may well have died in the same horrid fashion as his mother did. You'd be pretty angry too, wouldn't you? Wouldn't you want to try and stop it all?"

"These red files are 'Eyes Only', you know that."

"Yes I know but, I only read that one," she said, pointing to the one he was still trying to read. "The other one looked like just a list of places. I was bored waiting. I'd have been waiting still had I not decided to use my own car. Anyway I have the clearance," she said, re-affirming her position and her authority.

"I suppose you have, but, Eyes Only means Eyes Only."

"Oh don't be so bloody pompous. You sound just like Father." Angela handed back the photocopy to Lawson without any further comment on its content. She looked at her wrist watch; analogue, diamond encrusted, platinum cased, expensive and a present from him. "We had better get going, or we will miss our flight."

"Now just a minute, you are not going up there with me. This is a sanitation problem that could turn out very messy even if handled correctly." Lawson did not want to elaborate knowing she'd had feelings for Lomas in the past.

"Spare me the euphemisms. You don't have to kill him. If you can get me close enough to him I may be able to talk some sense into him. I am going with you and that is that," she added, emphatically.

"What would Sir Geoffrey say if I were to allow it?"

"I don't give a stuff what Father thinks or you for that matter. I am the only one of the lot of you who really knows Eric." She could feel herself getting flushed, and hoped Lawson hadn't noticed.

"You still have feelings for him, after all this time." There was disappointment in Lawson's voice.

"Yes, of course. Like a brother really, that's all. I gave up any other hopes when he married Katherine. I despise him in truth. I despise him for turning against my father, who took him in when there was no one else. I despise him for turning against his friends and colleagues and all the reasons he did the job. I despise him most for turning against his country, but that doesn't mean I want to kill him. I just look at what has pushed him to this. I don't want you to kill him because, I love him. I don't want you to kill him because I love you, and you are my soul-mate, silly." She reached out and touched his hand. "You don't have to kill him."

"But there is only one place booked on the flight," Lawson argued.

"Then use your authority and get me a seat next to yours, darling. I'm going, and that is final."

They left the diner together and Lawson drove them to Henlow airfield in his car. Lawson had no difficulty getting Angela past security and onto the base. He showed his D1 clearance pass and the guard immediately snapped to attention and raised the barrier. However, the pilot of the small jet aircraft standing by to fly him to Cumbria refused point blank to take an extra passenger, even when she too had produced a D1 clearance pass.

"Jane has already filed the fight plan with control and there's only enough fuel aboard for us and one passenger," he stressed in a clipped precise manner, audible above the piecing whistle of his aircraft's enthusiastic jet engines.

"Listen to me carefully, Rogers," Lawson shouted calmly; the pilot's name was stitched above the left breast pocket of his flight-suit. "We both go. Do I make myself clear? Or do I need to disturb the minister and explain to him how your reluctance may have cost us the success of our mission? We are both going, even if Jane has to remain here."

"But he's my navigator, I don't fly without him," the pilot replied, less self-assured than he at first appeared. "He is my eyes and ears as it were."

"Then an alternative solution is to be found, don't you agree?" Lawson was insistent.

"Indeed, sir. Might I suggest in that case, you and the young lady climb aboard and make yourselves comfortable and I'll discuss an alternative plan with Flight Lieutenant Russell?"

"Thank you, Captain Rogers, this would seem to be the most sensible way to proceed. Angela after you." Lawson held out his hand and helped her onto the first step and followed her up into the twin engine Hawker Siddeley jet which sat with its engines already whining and straining to release their pent up thrust and propel the plane into the skies like a silver bullet.

There were two rows of five seats, facing each other along the sides of the fuselage. A long low box, like a coffee table, which extended along the middle of the cabin floor in front of these, was the only adornment other than the seats.

Captain Rogers secured the outer door and stepped into the cockpit to prepare for take-off. A moment or two later he reappeared, smiling. "We have been given a new flight plan. We were to take you to RAF Kingstown but there will be no car there for you, so we are to take you to RAF Cockermouth instead, where there will be a company car waiting for you on the apron. As Cockermouth is that much nearer Jane says we have enough fuel for one more passenger, provided she is under fifteen stones, which I assured him you are, madam."

"Thank you, Captain," said Angela.

"Ladies and gentlemen, we are just now cleared for take off. However, I must apologise that due to the brevity of our flight today, which Jane assures me will be a measly but interesting thirty-five minutes, there will be no inflight movie. Please would you now buckle up seat belts straight away, securely stow all hand luggage and ensure your tray tables are in the upright position during take-off," said Captain Rogers with a smile of such genuine insincerity that they all laughed and an air of friendliness broke out.

"Your navigator, Lieutenant Russell?" queried David Lawson.

"Yes, ask me anything you like. We were at Cranwell together," Captain Rogers replied.

"Then you might have chosen a better nickname for him. Jack or even Bertrand at a pinch, but Jane? Seems a bit mean," said Lawson. They laughed again.

"Not at all, in fact it suits him rather well. You haven't met him, have you? He likes to be a bit of a drama queen at times." Captain Rogers giggled at the thought and disappeared into the cockpit, leaving Lawson and Angela sniggering in their belted seats.

"This lot seem to have a good time," Angela commented.

"Yeh. I wonder what Jane Russell is really like though, probably a techno-nerd." Lawson did not need to wonder for long.

The aircraft began to move forward towards the runway and over the cabin loudspeakers came the voice of the navigator and co-pilot, Jane Russell. "Welcome aboard, ladies and gentlemen. We will be travelling subsonic today at a height of twenty-nine thousand feet and at a cruising speed of five hundred and eighty miles per hour. When we hit turbulence if you find all your small change has fallen out of your pockets do not be alarmed as this is not an unusual phenomenon when flying upside down. This is a manoeuvre your pilot today sometimes uses to stabilise the plane and welcome new passengers." Click, the speakers turn off. Lawson and Angela Fenton could hear Lieutenant Russell and Captain Rogers laughing loudly behind the closed cockpit door. Click, speakers back on again: "Hold on to your lunch here we go." Click!

And with a sudden and thrilling increase in the volume of its roaring jet engines the small aircraft shot forward, rotated and pushed itself up against and over the hardening column of air beneath its rigid wings. In an instant they were through the low cloud and into bright dazzling sunlight that hurt their eyes as it streamed into the cabin through the five portholes on each side of the plane's fuselage.

Lawson reached inside his jacket with his left hand. The Sig Sauer nine millimetre pistol and silencer rested easily in its thin cloth holster under his right armpit. He felt more comfortable with it there, even though he was hoping now he would have no need to use it with Angela there. She had placed the attaché case in front of him but he was in no mood for reading any more depressing material. Not after the comedy duo had done such good work cheering him up.

"There's one place up there that he is bound to go," suggested Angela, seeing his mood was now less stressed. She wanted to help him as much as possible and justify her presence.

"One that jumps out at you, I know," said Lawson. "I thought you didn't read the list?"

"I didn't. I just scanned it, that's all. It's not even on the list anyway." Angela held her companion in suspense.

"Well, I am listening. It can't be the old lab. He knows that would be too obvious, and it's on the list," said Lawson.

"But that's not where I was thinking he'll go. We'll try there too, he may go there as well."

"As well as where?"

"Her grave. Ilyana's grave. He will definitely go there. His father is there too," said Angela in triumph.

"My God, you're right. Well done. We'll go there first; see if there is any evidence of him being there, you know, footprints."

"Flowers," Angela interrupted.

"Yes, that sort of thing." Lawson was excited. Now he had the scent. "Where is it, the grave?"

"Ah. I don't know, but it's in the files. Bessomethwaite can't be more than a small village with two churches at most. We could ask when we check in with the local police." Lawson looked doubtfully at her following this suggestion. "We are going to check in with the locals, aren't we?" she asked.

"Well, your father considered it would be a bad idea to get them too involved initially, at least not before I, or rather we now can locate him and assess the level of risk he poses."

"Oh great, that means we'll have no protection."

"Time is not on our side and the fuse is getting shorter. We must locate him as quickly as possible, ascertain the threat and maybe then we can speak to the locals. We'll see."

"Then, in my opinion, there is only one place, one asset we have up there he could damage enough to make political waves, assuming, what must be obvious now, he does not wish to open the vials in any populated area." Angela sat back in her seat as if she had just finished *The Times* crossword.

"The new National Biochemical Research Facility, under Benlow's Fell."

"Has to be our first port of call," agreed Angela.

"You said you just scanned that list."

"Yes, but I am a fast reader."

The remainder of their flight, what there was of it, passed without incident or further comment from either passengers or crew. All were locked in a silence which seemed to Lawson to grow darker the longer it continued. Angela refused to meet his occasional glances and entertainment from the cockpit had ceased. Lawson could feel a gradual building-up of tension twisting tighter and tighter like a rubber band inside him, increasing until the moment of its release in a spinning explosion of unravelling events. It had always been like this for him at the start of a mission. The senses of excitement and foreboding, each surging with equal force through his entire system, would appear to telegraph a message to others around him that they should leave him to his thoughts as he picked through his final plans for the impending action. Usually he worried about the many things that could go wrong. He would always try to imagine alternatives to the plan that would guarantee success; but not this day.

Lawson contemplated the delicate balance in which fate now held his own mortality, now he also had Angela's welfare to consider. He became suddenly conscious of the possibility he may very well survive this encounter with Eric. Years before he had adopted a fatalistic outlook towards his chances against Eric. In training Eric was always faster, more accurate, more ruthless, more everything really. But Lomas must be a little rusty from his nearly eight months now out of ops. Lawson believed he could take him down now, if he had to. If he couldn't: well it wouldn't really matter much anymore because he'd be shot to hell and dead instead.

He turned over in his mind what would happen if his mission did succeed. How would Angela react if he did take Eric down, stop him dead? What would Angela do when Lomas was dead, when Eric was actually laying dead or dying on the ground, Eric's noble head in her lap, but the weapon which finally despatches Lomas and saves Western civilization as we know it is there, still smoking his hand. What will Angela see then, a gallant saviour or a callous state's assassin?

He guessed either would eventually herald the end of their relationship. Even though she was unaware Lomas was her half-brother, David Lawson knew she thought of him in those terms. It would only be a question of time, no matter how she viewed him after the event. He had to admit to himself it would be hard to return from a mission that had resulted in him killing her only brother and for them then to carry on their relationship from where they were before, let alone as if nothing had happened. The very fact that now she would probably be there to witness the action first-hand seemed to make their eventual break-up even more inevitable.

And then he felt the jets reduce their thrust and wisps of white cloud began to flash past the portholes and darken the cabin; they had begun their descent.

Captain Rogers' slow deep voice came over the loudspeakers, "Ladies and gentlemen we have begun our descent into Cockermouth," followed by:

"OOH-ER, Missus." Obviously Flight Lieutenant Jane's contribution.

175

"Please put out all your fags," Captain Rogers suggested in a mild manner.

"As the management frown on any kind of elitist or sexually deviant behaviour," said Jane, hitting his stride.

"And fasten your seat belts, please."

"Yes I would if I were you. We have very little fuel left now for what we like to call a textbook controlled landing so we're going to try gliding in on the thermals." He couldn't help himself giggling at the thought of that. Flight Lieutenant Russell, although a dedicated professional and serious about the important work he and his pilot did, also believed that humour was a main source of good health and mental balance and who is to say he is wrong?

"This is Captain Rogers signing off and may I take this opportunity to thank you for flying FunAir.gov and join with my navigator Flight Lieutenant Jane Russell in wishing you a pleasant onward journey," said Captain Rogers finally. The engines roared into reverse thrust and the small jet aircraft touched down on the tarmac as softly as if it were an Apollo moon-landing capsule.

Chapter Fifteen

Enemy Within

Killing an armed police officer was a mistake, unavoidable, but it had been a mistake nonetheless. Lomas, unfortunately, had reacted purely from instinct when disarming the officer, pulling him through the opened driver's window into the car in one smooth swift movement, and shooting him twice in the back of the head. The first shot had not killed the officer, his legs and feet had continued jerking sporadically through the open window, but the second to the base of the skull had. They would guess it had been him, no doubt, when they found the body.

Lomas knew how lucky he had been getting as far from Weymouth as he had without being spotted. He should have dumped the car he had stolen from the university much sooner. But it had taken him all the way up the spine of England, through the Midlands and into Cumbria. It was unlucky though that the officer, who had eventually pulled him over, had been an armed response officer. Had it been otherwise Lomas would probably have been able to talk his way out of an arrest or, at the very least, disable the officer before commandeering his unmarked pursuit vehicle. Unlucky for the officer too, if he had known with whom he was dealing he would not have arrogantly waved his hand gun so close to Lomas's face.

On the back seat of the Fiesta he had stolen in Weymouth, Lomas found various items of clothing. Among the belongings of the students who owned the car were two dark navy overcoats. He tried on the smaller of the two. It was a little too big for him and the sleeves hung down below his clenched hands, but the material was thick and warm. Perfect, it could also serve as a blanket if he was going to sleep rough that night. The larger of the two coats he used to cover the body of the dead officer. Leaving the body and the stolen car well concealed in shrubbery by the roadside, he quietly drove off in the unmarked police car.

Fatigue soon began to rake his body. He had driven all that day from the south coast in the little Fiesta, amid the detritus of student life: crushed beer cans, empty pizza boxes, textbooks, various articles of clothing and foot-ware. The smells of damp sweaty clothes, cigarettes, alcohol and grease-laden takeaways were overpowering but not nearly as repugnant to Lomas as the fetid back streets of Baghdad where he had been only a few days before. Keeping well under the speed limits to avoid being spotted it had been a long drive. He was tired and hungry and getting the stolen Fiesta far enough into the bushes so as not to be seen easily from the road had nearly finished him. He needed to find somewhere safe to stop and rest. He decided he would eat something after he had rested.

He guessed it would be some time before the students' stolen Fiesta and the body of the policeman were found. The Club would know it was him when the reports came in, then he would have to move quickly. But if he wanted to complete his own planned mission, he had to rest. He was very close now to his objective but they would close in quickly once they guessed his target. A few hours were probably all he had, he could not tell, but he needed to get some sleep. So, he drove towards the place where, really, it had all begun, to where he had played in happier times. The place where he would wait for his mother to finish her experiments, where he would wait for her to take him home. They would chat about his day, never about her work, she always left that behind with her white lab coat. She would tell him stories from her homeland while she prepared their evening meal and later sing him Hungarian lullabies that whispered like a summer's breeze through the soft grasses of the sun-warmed meadows of his sleep. How he missed her; he missed that sweet voice.

He left the silver grey police Sierra a mile or so back along the narrow, overgrown track. Although he doubted anyone had used the path for years, he thought it more prudent to be well away from the car if it were discovered by chance before daybreak. The bushes and trees pushed into him and bore down onto him from above as he forged his way between them towards the buildings he knew were there at the end of the lane. He had not expected them to be so dilapidated. The old place, surrounded by tall pines and a high fence had decayed somewhat during its half century of neglect. The lower branches of the trees had grown out thickly and densely through the rusty chainlink fence, and in places had pushed through and snapped the brittle brown metal. He walked slowly up to the old crumbling wire gate and rubbed his hand over the large metal sign that hung from it. Small chunks of rust and silver paint snowed down in a flurry over his rough brown desert shoes but the sign's message was still legible.

Property of HM Ministry of Defence.
Bessomthwaite 288
Trespassers Will Be Prosecuted

There was also a more recent and less equivocal statement on a newer plaque fixed below. This one proclaimed: 'No

Unauthorised Admittance by Order of MOD. Persons Ignoring This Order Risk a Long Prison Sentence'. Moreover, the new sign gave an emergency telephone number at the bottom and the name of the nearest hospital, which implied, anyone ignoring the sign above may well need to obtain immediate medical attention. He wondered why the people at the Ministry of Defence had not thought just giving the hospital's name and telephone number would have been a sufficient deterrent, without the added threat of prison. It would certainly have made him think twice about risking a forced entry, had he been at all concerned about his own continuing good health that is. He scaled the gate easily and dropped down onto the overgrown shingled path on the other side.

Most of the out buildings: catering, office, and wash houses were demolished down to the foundations but the main laboratory building was still pretty much in tact. Windows were broken here and there and it looked generally dilapidated, but the roof was still mostly in place. He could do little better than to overnight there if he wished to remain undetected. He found a huge newish looking padlock securing the main doors. *They must still be checking the place then*, he thought. Undeterred, Lomas picked the lock and quietly slid inside, silently closing the metal door behind him.

Although his eyes quickly became accustomed to the level of the darkness inside, it still took him a while to make out the lines of the benches and cabinets in the cold dank eerie space before him. He stumbled about, not knowing the layout of things. He had never been allowed in the laboratories when he was a boy. He found two rotting easy chairs that he guessed his mother and father would have used. He pushed them together and lay down across them, totally exhausted.

As tired as he was he found it difficult to sleep, not even the memory of his mother's soft voice could lull him at first. He lay there warm in the thick blanket of his borrowed naval overcoat, stretched between the two armchairs staring into the blackness. He watched small puffs of cloud drift slowly past a patch of stars that pieced a hole in the broken ceiling above his face. A clear night he thought, thankfully. He was far too tired to even think of moving.

He remembered the history of the place he was in and began to imagine the gruesome deaths inflicted on so many of the animal inhabitants of the facility but eventually the clouds and stars gave way to dreams. He slept only in fits and starts and woke several times during the night, each time disturbed by a different but gruesome remembered nightmare; of Katherine and the boys, or his mother and the man he still thought of as his father. Seeing it as if it was happening right in front of him he witnessed the hopeless and pain filled decline of his mother into death and understood his father's helplessness and anguish. Lomas had carried a suppressed guilt since learning the truth about her death, which in his dreams that night found new levels of intensity and he began to understand why his father had taken his own life shortly after. Unable, as he had been, to help her in her final torment, he had succumbed to the very demons that were now telling Lomas to self-destruct.

At one point a clear image of the man Lomas most hated appeared as clear as if standing before him. The spectre tried to excuse itself for its deception while slowly transforming itself into a large mythical snake-like monster, from which Lomas recoiled. The features possessed by this fantastical beast were the unmistakeable features possessed by Sir Geoffrey Fenton.

He woke fully in a sudden jolt and with pale sunlight creeping in dull shafts through the shattered window panes which faced east. He had woken refreshed, despite his disturbed night, and very hungry. He urinated into a cracked basin by the door but no water came from either tap when he tried them. He washed his hands in some standing water that had collected in a shallow pool on one of the lab benches. He wiped his wet hands across his face and dried them under his armpits.

He had woken too with a determination, not only to complete his mission, but to survive the enterprise and return to France and to happiness ever after. He knew very well happy ever after was usually confined to fairy tales, but his remembered dreams from the night before had left him with an overwhelming feeling of hope and expectation rather than doom.

This morning he must dispose of the police Sierra more carefully than he was able to hide the student's stolen Fiesta the previous evening. So just after dawn he drove the Sierra across rough country, off road in search of a body of water deep enough for his purpose. Under its sheen, the water of the little tarn that glinted before him could have been deep enough to hide an aircraft carrier in, never mind a car. It seemed to shelve suddenly just a foot or two from the sloping bank where he stood. If the car went down without a trace and remained unseen from the air, that may give him all the time he required.

Lomas looked in the boot and prized open the weapons cabinet secured there. He took nothing from it other than a Glock 17 semi-automatic pistol and two clips of nine-millimetre ammunition, even though the metal cabinet revealed a cache of heavy weaponry of every description. These contents, he calculated, would give the car more weight and help it to sink. Besides, what ever he took now he would have to carry cross-country on the hike he had planned. The gun had no silencer. Armed police, he reasoned, would obviously prefer the noise unsuppressed guns make as it would tend to warn off any innocent bystanders. Although Lomas preferred to use the suppressed Sig Sauer weapons the Club usually provided, this Glock would do the job he wanted. He shoved it, and the two clips, into a pocket of his greatcoat.

Toying with the idea of using an item of police overt body armour for some protection, he considered the fundamental elements of his own training and experience: body shots to disable, arms and legs to restrain and deter, head shots to terminate. They were trained to aim for the mouth of a human target; two shots. With luck one round would sever the spinal cord and prevent the hostile's hand receiving the 'pull the trigger' message from his brain. Lomas decided the vest would probably be unnecessary.

He jerked the handbrake of the silver grey Sierra free. He pushed the car forwards towards the edge of the little mere. It rolled slowly at first down the gentle slope, gradually picking up speed. Into and under the water it slid, sending deep ripples across the flat placid lake. The silver car slowly disappeared beneath the surface of the water like a large ingot of grey steel melting into grey metallic liquid. The water bubbled for a short time as if boiling. Steam rose from the spitting hissing centre of the cauldron as the hot engine met the cold water and the exhaust pipe snapped and crackled before finally disappearing into the cold depths.

There was no wind to speak of now and the water soon regained its original composure. Caught in the grey light of early dawn, the small mere was once more like a shining solid metal slab. Not a breath of wind ruffled its surface. The water looked cold and hard, hard enough to carve a name in. The brave sun of first light began to pale and disappear. A featureless grey sky fell down upon the now shapeless grey hills and blurred their timeless majesty into one grey smudge.

Lomas stared blankly at the expanse of water before him, expecting nothing from its sheen other than the gradual appearance of his own name being written there, fatefully, by some unseen hand. Instead a light breeze got up and blew a fan of ripples wide and whimsically before it, with no design, no striking of Lomas across the tarn's monolithic surface. It was not fate that drove him to this place beneath Benlow's Fell, nor destiny; it was his own will, his own all consuming desire for retribution, his own intention to stop it all, to end the madness and begin his own redemption.

This was to be his last mission. He could then disappear for good and lead a normal, happy life of peaceful obscurity. But he had to play this one out to the bitter end now whether it was to be just his final mission or in fact his final act in life. Lomas had asked himself before he left France whether they would want to take him or kill him and he had conceded that, for them, there were no options. No fuss, no embarrassing enquiry, no mess. They would have to kill him. He, however, had other plans for his retirement.

He smiled to himself. In the Club he was known as 'No Mess Lomas'. As their top field officer he had proven always to be a safe yet deadly pair of hands. Every mission of his executed with a lethal professionalism and he never left a trail of bloody footprints that could lead back to the department and, more importantly, to the government officials who gave him sanction. But this, this was so different that it was unlikely any of them would anticipate it; he was truly changed. They may still be expecting him to target London if they hadn't yet found the Fiesta and the dead body of the policeman, but he quickly concluded that was unlikely too.

He was certain Club members would have already been unleashed and set to find him. The department would try to track him at first but then as a wider risk evaluation was established others would try to stop him and the only way to do that would be to eliminate him. Once loosed from their slips, his comrades in arms would become the very hounds now sent to hunt him down and finish him. But he reasoned if they had not predicted his target, they would not yet have plans in place to counteract his threat and that might just give him the time he needed to complete this last mission and escape undetected. But he could not afford any more mistakes. Lomas knew he had an opportunity to deliver a message. A subtle but loud message to the government and the rest of the world perhaps, a message to which they would have to give some attention.

He carried in his pocket, still, the camera which contained in two vials a small quantity of pathogen Bessomthwaite 288, enough he assessed, to wipe out all breathing life in Northern England and probably the Midlands; that was, if it were in the wrong hands. He was attempting to bring it home, return it to the very place it was produced and release it where it would do the most harm and yet be the least devastating. Too many people had died already due to its virulence, and died horrible deaths. Some of these people were people whom he had loved the most. Warfare of this unholy nature had to be stopped before mankind wiped itself from the face of the planet. Since making his mind shattering discovery in the desert the week before he was resolved to use the means he had found in Iraq to put a stop to the British biological and chemical warfare programme for good. It did not occur to him that he might unknowingly be acting as an agent for a foreign power, nor would it have worried him if he had. His motives, as he saw them, were of the most honourable.

It began to rain. It was only a light rain at first but it was a ubiquitous rain. It fell on the water and suddenly dulled the shining surface of the lake with its innumerable needle like pinpricks. It was the kind of innocuous rain that could eventually soak into your skin. It fell straight down between the branches of the trees, between the twigs, between the rusting leaves. It seeped into the fabric of his coat. It trickled through the hair on his head. It ran down the back of his neck to his shoulders and down his back. It was a rain that could sap a man's motivation, drain a man's will, snuff out a man's determination. Lomas however was a different kind of man. He found the rain refreshed him.

He pulled up the collar of his greatcoat and considered his next decision. As with all the decisions he had made recently, once made, his options seemed suddenly to diminish. Had they found the dead police officer and the other car yet? Would they have worked out his intentions? Would they have guessed where he was about to strike? Would they be waiting there for him, and would they manage to end him before the last act? He tried to think where he could lay a dead trail, but he knew he would have no time for that. So what were his options now?

He remembered suddenly that he was hungry. He needed food, as soon as possible. He felt weakened, even though he had managed some sleep at the old laboratory. He needed something more than sleep now to sustain him. But first he would pay his respects to the woman who unwittingly set these events in motion. At the grave of his dear mother, in the little grave-yard of St John's Chapel under Benlow's Fell by Bessomthwaite he would secure his salvation.

Chapter Sixteen

In Bessomthwaite

The small village of Bessomthwaite is little more than a hamlet. It has a village hall and a pub. It has a petrol garage which also serves as the village shop and post office. Just out of the village there is the solitary Victorian chapel of St John's, but there is little else that would encourage anyone other than the five hundred inhabitants of Bessomthwaite to bestow on this collection of dwellings beside its eponymous lake any classification other than hamlet.

There is no school in Bessomthwaite, for instance. There is no police house either. There is a house called 'The Old Police House' which was purchased as an abandoned building by yuppies in the early eighties and converted into a modern palace of stainless steel and venetian blinds, which is how it remains. The nearest police station now is Keswick.

Lawson and Angela were shown into the Assistant Chief Constable's office. They shook hands and the ACC asked them both to sit down.

"Sir," Lawson began, "I believe our governor has been in contact with you regarding our dilemma."

"Yes, well the Chief Constable spoke to Sir Geoffrey directly but he has related to me the gist of their conversation."

"Good, very good," said Lawson, surprised that the lines of communication between departments seemed to be working so efficiently. But he was all too soon to be disappointed.

"Then you will have already suspended your investigations into the killing of your armed officer as requested?" he continued.

"I most certainly have not," the ACC assured him, arrogantly.

"What?" Lawson erupted. "Why in God's name not?"

"For the moment," the ACC began in reply. He had been surprised by the vehemence of Lawson's outburst and struggled with his words.

"We have very little to go on," he continued. "We are still looking for our vehicle you know."

Lawson was too annoyed to respond. He shook his head from side to side in disbelief.

"Look, you must understand that this is a murder investigation," the ACC went on. "The murder of a policeman, which we take very seriously indeed, and it could still be the case that the real culprit is someone other than your man."

"Don't you have tracking devices fitted to your vehicles, particularly armed response vehicles?" Angela asked.

"Yes, dear," replied the ACC. If he had added, 'don't you worry your pretty little head about it,' he could not have sounded more patronising. "Of course we do, but it has been disabled somehow and we haven't received a signal since yesterday evening."

Lawson and Angela looked at each other. Their thinking was going in the same direction. They were both convinced now that Lomas was indeed culpable for the demise of the policeman but to Angela's surprise Lawson took a different tack.

"You are right, we should not assume the murderer is our man, especially without any evidence. However, we need to find and eliminate Commander Lomas from your enquiries," affirmed Lawson, seemingly calm again.

"That is what we have been attempting to do. Once we have found him and questioned him you can have him. I can't call off a murder investigation at the drop of a hat," the ACC insisted.

"But you must for the safety of your other officers. This man can be extremely dangerous. Didn't your Chief Constable impress that upon you?" Lawson was getting agitated again.

"Yes he did, but you must know what governors are like, they seldom understand the logistics of a real situation. Most of my officers are out combing the area unpaid, in their spare-time. This is one of their own that's been murdered, you understand. I can't ask them to call off the search for evidence, and even if I could I doubt if many would respond positively. You do see my position don't you?"

"Oh, I understand all right, it is you who does not." Lawson was fuming, even though he was not unaware of the similarities in their respective situations. "This meeting was intended solely as a courtesy visit, to smooth any ruffled feathers there might be up here and to assure you that we have no intention of stepping on anyone's toes. Now I see that it was vital to impress on you the gravity of your situation. Let me make it quite clear. The damage this man can do here far surpasses the death of one policeman. You have no idea of the scale of threat you and your officers are likely to stumble upon. If any of your men spook this individual he could release Armageddon. Call them off now, immediately."

"Should I call Sir Geoffrey?" Angela suggested to David Lawson.

"Good idea, Miss Fenton, I'm sure he will be highly amused to find the level of indiscipline allowed in the ranks of the Keswick and Penrith Police Forces. I'm sure he will wish to bring this point to the attention of the Home Secretary when next they meet," Lawson added.

"Now now, let's not get too hasty." All colour had suddenly drained from the ACC's face as he saw his carefully engineered career disappearing like a snowball on a bonfire. "I seem to have given you the impression I intend to be obstructive here. Let me assure you, nothing could be further from the truth. But you can see my position, surely. I want this resolved quickly, as much as you seem to, but the police must be seen at least to have played a part in its resolution. Perhaps some of my better trained officers can assist you?" he offered, in a desperate attempt to regain some face and authority.

"That's very kind, but both Miss Fenton and I are fully trained and know the man. We have already identified several places we believe he may visit before he tries to disappear from our radar. He is unarguably our best operative and is a master in avoiding detection. This is best left completely to us." Lawson could see the ACC searching for some kind of compromise.

"I can't leave the thing that open ended. I must have something I can throw to the troops to placate them temporarily." He was clutching at straws now.

"Okay, we'll make a deal with you," offered Angela. "Give us a free hand for twenty-four hours, and if by then we have not located him we'll turn the whole thing over to you. Agreed?" Lawson turned his head and looked at her in astonishment, but relief had begun to replace mild panic on the ACC's face.

"I can live with that," he said. "Twenty-four hours you say, and any leads you uncover you bring directly to me. Yes?"

"Of course!" said Lawson quickly, backing Angela's play.

They left the office with the ACC already on the telephone to his operations centre. He was explaining carefully what he wanted to happen and how quickly he expected these things to occur.

Back in the car David Lawson breathed a heavy sigh of relief. Nevertheless he did have one small concern.

"Twenty-four hours and we share info, what did you say that for?"

"Well at least now we have a clear run," she explained.

"But share information, you know we can't do that."

"We won't have to. Look, in twenty-four hours if we haven't found him that will mean one of two things has happened. One is that he has left the area and this is not his intended target."

"And the second?"

"He has released the pathogen already. So it's not going to matter much what happens after that anyway. Everyone up here, including ourselves, will have all the information on his whereabouts they are ever likely to need. Now let's go follow up on your first hunch, the old lab."

"You're as slippery as a box of frogs, you," Lawson said, admiringly. "Got the map?"

"I have my moments," she agreed as she punched a grid reference into the satellite navigation device in the glove box.

"Drive on and at the end of this road turn right towards Bessomthwaite." She watched him turn the key and put the car into gear and she smiled. She was glad she was with him. The fact they might both be killed in the line of duty was a distinct possibility which only served to increase her desire to be there and to see this through with him. In that event her father would have to admire her dedication, at the very least.

"The new biotech facility is beneath the Benlow's Massive," she told him. "It's on the opposite side of the fell to the old post-war laboratories of Bessomthwaite 288. If his intended target is either of these, Bessomthwaite village is between the two. From Keswick he must pass through it on his way to either one. He wouldn't ever go through Bessomthwaite, I'm sure, without visiting the grave in St John's cemetery. Let's take a look there first, see if he has been about," she suggested.

"His mother's remains aren't there, he knows that." Lawson sounded sceptical.

"Yes, but still, it's got to be worth a look. We may find evidence that he's been there, that it is him and he is in the area."

"And if there isn't this evidence where are you then? Still hanging on to the thought it might not be Eric I suppose," Lawson enquired, a hint of jealousy creeping into his voice.

"No!" Angela replied quickly but she remained thoughtful and added, "No, not at all. In some respects I hope he is up here with the stuff and not down in London after Daddy. And that's not to mention the population of eastern England then being under threat of extinction."

"I take your point," said Lawson. Realising he was acting idiotically he drew her attention momentarily to the towering peaks on either side of the road. Their tops shrouded in low hanging cloud and he remarked, "We may yet manage to head him off at the pass."

"Sure thing, partner," she replied and touched his hand to reassure him of her.

They laughed together, both attempting to ease the other's growing anxieties.

The day, which had begun in sunshine and so positively for Lomas, had deteriorated somewhat. The shy rain of earlier had organised itself into a deluge of monsoon proportions making the mountain a most inhospitable place. Gills and becks which barely had an identity the day before sprang into life, cascading through once dry gullies and over mossy crags to the lower hills making each rock and boulder slippery and dangerous under foot. Experienced fell walkers remained in their warm dry lodges and hotel bars and prepared for an afternoon familiarising themselves from books with the relevant Wainwright Walk they might have enjoyed had the weather been less inclement. Even sheep, used to the violent extremes of weather in the fells, pushed themselves close to whatever shelter they could find and by all appearances seemed thoroughly sorry for themselves.

Lomas was indeed soaking and cold to the bone himself. He slithered down the wet shale. His suede boots, meant for desert wear not mountaineering, were sodden and slipped under him whenever he put a foot down without care. He had hiked up and over Benlow's Fell and fortunately had encountered no other walkers reckless enough to chance the daunting climb. It had been slow going it was true but he could see the chapel now and his spirit lifted again.

The small Presbyterian chapel of St John's and the dry-stone wall which surrounds it are made of the same grey, locally quarried granite as all the houses in the tiny hamlet of Bessomthwaite. The stone possesses a depressing sheen of darkness when damp. This dampness, drawn down by the surrounding hills from the oppressing clouds, seems to suffocate the place and renders it void of any sunlight or colour. In the tiny nooks and crannies between the chiselled stone boulders green lichens and mosses do grow, but even their striking verdancy offers little resistance to the overwhelming greyness of the stone.

He climbed over the low wall behind the chapel, at a place he could not be seen from the road and walked slowly through the soaked carpet of grass and fallen leaves to a wooden bench seat. The rain had all but stopped now, so he brushed aside some of the wet golden leaves that had fallen on the bench and sat down. A little way in front of where he sat, beside a cinder path, were several gravestones. He did not know the other people buried either side, but he guessed they would have known his mother and Dr Philip Lomas.

Lush, unkempt grass had grown over the grave. Just a plain stone of grey black granite marked the official resting place of the two people he had once loved more than any others in the whole wide world. Chiselled into the headstone were the words:

In Loving Memory of:

Prof. Ilyana Lomas
nee Kadich
1933 – 1972

Beloved of:
Dr. Philip Lomas
1929 – 1975

May they rest in peace, together forever.

Eric read these words again, as if for the first time. He sat with his head in his hands and remembering how in love they had been. He remembered that Sir Geoffrey Fenton had implied it was a bit over the top when suggesting that the punctuation points were unnecessary.

Eric realised now it wasn't those punctuation marks that had been bothering Fenton. It would have been more that he, Sir Geoffrey Fenton who had loved Ilyana too, was unable to express the true extent of his grief.

Eric had realised for a long while that at Ilyana's funeral no-one would have known he was in fact Fenton's boy, he hadn't even known himself then. Brigadier Geoffrey Fenton, as he had been then, would have had no idea either. Philip Lomas was still, as far as Eric knew then, his real father and neither of them were aware of Ilyana's affair with Fenton at that time.

Sitting reading those words again, the saddest words ever to come from the bottom of his soul, Eric felt glad Philip Lomas had brought him up and was still the only person he truly thought of as his father; he had been a good man. He knew in his innermost self how his mother and Philip Lomas had felt about each other. It had shown in the way they were with one another, how they were really and truly in love with each other. He knew this for sure now.

He thought a moment of Fabien, in France alone and anxious. He was certain the bond he had with her was the same elemental bond that had existed between his mother and Dr Philip Lomas. He sat for a time thinking of lost youth and the stark truth of the transitory nature of our existence, until he heard a car approach the front gate and continued past towards Keswick. This seemed to galvanize him into concerted action once more.

He walked across the cinder path to the grave and took from his pocket the small camera he had brought back from Iraq. Using one of the larger sharp flat stones which edged the cinder path he dug deep into the soil at the base of the headstone. Then, from a compartment of the camera intended to house batteries he removed one of the vials of Bessomthwaite 288. As if performing an ancient ritual, with great ceremony, he placed the vial gently into the hole and delicately replace the earth over it, muttering: "Earth to Earth, Ashes to Ashes, Dust to Dust."

Finally, he replaced the tuft of turf he had removed and trod it in lightly so as not to squash the grass too much. He added a light garnish of wet golden leaves, scattering just a few so there was no sign the ground had been disturbed. This was his insurance policy, in case some element of his plan went awry.

He heard another car approaching, from the south this time, but he did not wait for it to pass. He slipped quickly and quietly over the back wall of the cemetery and made for Bessomthwaite to find food and sustenance.

They drove slowly up to the gate of St John's Chapel. Lawson went to the boot and unlocked the weapons chest welded into the vehicle. He selected one of the five hand guns, checked the clip was full and slipped it into its holster under his jacket. He grabbed two shower-proof coats and handed one to Angela.

"Aren't you getting anything from the boot? he asked.

"No need. What's he going to do, shoot me?" she asked, rhetorically.

The wood and metal of the gate and its latch were slippery with wet moss. Lawson closed the gate behind them and wiped slimy lichens from his hand onto the sleeve of his jacket. He checked the gun in its holster one more time. Not that he was nervous, but doing so was reassuring.

Their boots crunched along the cinder path, up past the chapel and they approached the grave of Professor Ilyana Lomas. They both walked round the headstone searching for any trace of recent disturbance. They both showed their respect and were careful not to stand on the grave itself.

"Looks okay to me," Angela said.

"Yes," agreed Lawson. "Doesn't look as if anyone has been here for years. We still have Biotech."

"What about the old laboratories? We could try there," Angela suggested.

"Little point. The site is derelict now by all accounts, an unlikely target I would think."

They turned to go when Lawson noticed the leaves on the wooden bench, or rather the lack of them.

He stepped smartly across the cinder path and stared at the wet wood of the seat. There before him plainly visible on the wooden seat was a semi-circle of dryness. Surrounded by shiny dampness and wet leaves this one patch of wood was completely bone dry and unmistakably the shape that would be left by a person's backside.

"Someone has sat here, look," he shouted in his excitement. They both stared down at the dull patch of dried wood.

"Yes, and recently too," Angela added, mirroring his exhilaration. "It has only just stopped raining, had you noticed?"

Lawson placed his hand on the seminal half moon of dry wood. He then placed the other hand on the wet wood outside the arch. One hand felt warm as flesh and the other; cold as stone.

"My God, he is here. It's still warm. It has to be him. He sat here no more than a couple of minutes ago; feel," he commanded.

She felt the warmth of the wooden seat where, only a few moments before, Lomas had indeed sat. She turned quickly and called out his name but her voice was blown away eastwards by the westerly wind along with a small cloud of fluttering brown and gold leaves from the flapping, swaying trees.

"Check inside the chapel, but I think he must have heard us coming up the path. He's gone," said Lawson, serious now.

A quick turn around the chapel building, along the cinder path revealed nothing. Lawson's attempt to search the chapel for their man only served to confirm further they were indeed there alone. He found the doors to be firmly and securely locked against any unwarranted entry. A more graphic indicator of the decline in England's moral integrity Lawson was unwilling to contemplate. Evidently the desecration of church property was not confined solely to the urban areas of the country.

"We aren't that far from Biotech now. If he is this close and on foot, as I think he must be, we have a good chance of overtaking him and getting in position before he does," Angela said.

They returned to the car and Lawson secured his weapon in the boot safe before driving off towards Bessomthwaite.

Eric Lomas had purchased a packet of crisps and a pork pie from the village shop post office and garage. He stood now in the doorway of the shop taking large bites from the pie and crunching down a handful of cheese and onion with growing satisfaction.

The car passed him at speed and although he recognised only Angela initially, he guessed it must be David Lawson in there with her. Eric Lomas watched as their car carried on away and up the street, still unsure whether they had seen him there in the shop doorway. He had turned up the collar of his greatcoat earlier against the wet west wind which now blew wildly between the crouching cottages of the hamlet. The coat which had been too big for him from the outset may have assisted in him avoiding their attention and he sank into it a little more. They could have missed spotting him.

Then suddenly red brake lights glared on, adding a warm blush to the cold, wet, monochrome street. He watched the car veer to the curb and stop not more than two hundred yards from him. He was convinced by this they had seen him. He could see Lawson on the carphone, talking animatedly with someone, beating his free hand on the dashboard once or twice to emphasise the urgency of the situation. Lomas assumed Lawson was marshalling more troops to close him down completely.

"Shit!" Lomas spat out the word. The Club had done well to track him here, he had to concede, but it was unlucky for him to have walked out right in front of them as he had. Nothing he could do about that now but react to the situation as he saw it. Perhaps he might be able to turn this apparent set back to his advantage.

Angela had been talking, not watching the street. She had missed Lomas in the doorway of the shop. David Lawson was listening, driving and watching each side of the road at once and he too had missed Lomas leaving the shop. It was at that precise moment Lawson's mobile telephone sprang audibly into life with Eric Clapton's classic opening riff to 'Motherless Children'.

"Hold on," he warned, and steered the car to the kerb and stopped with a jolt that pushed Angela forward in her seat.

Angela was about to ask who it was on the phone when Lawson, holding up a hand to her, spoke into the device in his other hand.

"Yes, hello Sir Geoffrey."

Lawson held his hand to Angela still. She could hear the voice speaking to Lawson but was unable to make out the words being said.

"In Bessomthwaite, sir," said Lawson in answer to Fenton's obvious question. There followed a short pause.

"Well, yes, sir, she is," Lawson admitted, answering another of Sir Geoffrey Fenton's self evident questions. A longer pause followed this answer and Angela could hear her father's voice; shouting now.

Lawson slapped the top of the dashboard with his free hand.

"Yes I..." The dashboard received another whack.

Fenton would not give Lawson a chance to interrupt. There followed an even longer pause as Sir Geoffrey read Lawson the riot act.

"But I..." David began, then yet another long pause. Sir Geoffrey's voice had moderated to quiet but serious instruction.

Angela attempted to interrupt but David's free hand, upheld once more, was enough for her to hold her tongue if not curb her impatience.

"But we can't let them deal with this. I've already explained to the Assistant Chief Commissioner; Lomas is our man. We owe Eric some professional courtesy, surely?" Lawson pleaded.

Pause.

"Yes of course I understand, but this doesn't sit well with me," Lawson complained. Fenton said something else now to Lawson, even more quietly, at the end of which Lawson replied, "Yes, sir, I'll be sure to tell her." He switched off the phone.

"Tell me what?" Angela asked.

"That was your father and he's less than pleased you are here."

"I gathered. His little baby in harm's way. Goodness whatever next?" She pouted and pretended to sulk. "So what is it you have got to tell me?" she enquired.

"That's what he wanted me to tell you and how I must stress to you that it has nothing to do with you being here that we are recalled to London immediately. We are to turn this back over to the locals, by ministerial order." Lawson's voice was filled with indignation.

"You're joking?"

"No. I wish I was. The minister has had second thoughts and backed out of any direct action which might backfire onto him. We are to let things take their natural course. Your father is livid. He is convinced the minister has not grasped the enormity of the amount of shit the government will be in if even a whiff of this were to leak. It will mean Brits at war in Iraq for sure. We'll have no way of holding back the Yanks and being sucked into it ourselves."

"Because we'll no longer have a legitimate reason not to join in," Angela added, finishing his point succinctly.

"I see you have been paying attention."

"One of my endearing qualities," Angela remarked. "Shame, we were so close at the cemetery, I could have talked him down, I am sure of it."

At that moment Angela's side of the car seemed to grow suddenly darker, as if a darker cloud had drifted across all the others, as if a great shadow had moved close to that side of their car. She turned her head towards the window to see the front of a very large and wet black coat pressed up against the glass and nothing else, nothing else that is except the non-silenced muzzle of a nine millimetre Glock 17 semi-automatic pistol. The gun, gripped by a pale hand protruding from the right sleeve of the coat, was pointed directly at her forehead.

"Stay very still both of you," Eric Lomas ordered. "I'm going to get into the back seat. Don't do anything dangerous or sudden, David, it would prove fatal for at least one of you." Lomas climbed into the back seat of the car and held the pistol to the back of David Lawson's head. In a low and menacing voice Lomas said one word only.

"Drive!"

They had not gone far before Lomas, still holding the Glock to the nape of Lawson's neck, reached into the front of the car and across Lawson's chest searching beneath his jacket for the gun that was always under Lawson's right arm. He remembered Lawson was left handed.

"Where's the Sig?" Lomas demanded on finding the holster there empty.

"In the boot, as per regulations," Lawson explained.

"And yours?" He directed the question towards Angela.

"The same," she replied, her voice tiny in terror. "Eric can't…"

"Well aren't you a couple of goodie goodie health and safety fanatics," Lomas mocked, not allowing Angela to finish.

They came to a T-junction where the road leaving the village meets the main road to Keswick. Lawson stopped the car.

"Where are we going?" he asked.

"I think the new place don't you? Biotech Life Sciences, isn't that where you were heading?" Lomas asked Angela. "I see you have it set already on your satnav there." He pointed to the small illuminated screen propped up in the opened glove box.

"Seems a good place for what you are carrying," Lawson ventured.

"You know, I thought that," Eric agreed. "Do you think they will let us in?" he asked quietly.

Lawson noticed then that Lomas was sounding too cool for the situation and recognised the likelihood of him becoming unstable very quickly. He needed to be handled.

"Are you okay, old man?" Lawson asked.

"I am fine. Don't you worry about me, you just worry about how to get us into Biotech without causing an international incident, old boy," he replied sarcastically.

They turned right at the junction, away from Bessomthwaite, towards the northern slopes of Benlow's Fell and the new underground biological research facility of Biotech Life Sciences.

Chapter Seventeen

At Barrow Beck Gate

They left the main road and took a narrow track sign-posted to Barrow Beck Farm. Lawson stopped the car.

"This doesn't look right to me," he said, shaking his head.

"Satnav says one point eight miles to destination along this track. Perhaps the sign is just there to deter any unwelcome visitors," Angela suggested.

"Keep going." Lomas pushed the gun into Lawson's neck to remind him it was still there. "If she has put in the right grid reference, it will be there."

Five minutes more and they came to a high grey reinforced-concrete wall. Spanning the track and barring their progress was a tall wide metal gate. Thick steel pillars supported either end of the solid, heavy looking gate and a bright metal intercom device was set into one of these. There were no signs to identify what lay beyond the gate, nor were there any instructions showing how to operate the intercom itself. A closed circuit television camera perched on top of the opposite pillar followed them as they approached and only when the car came finally to a halt, just a few feet away from the gate, did it stop its sweep. It watched and waited for any small sign of movement, like a hawk on a roadside pylon.

It was Angela who stepped gingerly from the car, responding to a barked instruction from Lomas. She walked slowly across the track to the bright stainless steel intercom. The camera tracked her as she did so and it stopped the moment she did. She could not escape the feeling that unexpected visitors were not welcomed here. She suspected that access to whatever lay beyond the gate would only be with prior consent but she pressed the square button on the keypad anyway in a vain hope for some response. When none was immediately forthcoming she pressed again and then again. She took a deep breath and was about to speak into the small circular grille above the keypad when a pleasant male voice spoke loudly to her from it.

"Just speak clearly into the grille if you would please, madam. What business do you have here?" the man's disembodied yet pleasant voice enquired.

"We are three national security officers on urgent and secret work for the Home Office. We must have access to your facility on a matter of immediate national importance," Angela pleaded rather lamely, but it was the best she could do on the fly.

"Who do you imagine we are?" the lulling, soporific voice asked sardonically.

"Biotech Life Sciences."

"No, that is not us I am afraid. Goodbye." The intercom clicked off and the voice was silenced, but the camera stayed where it was: watching her.

"Hello!" she shouted into the grille. "Hello!"

There was no response. Angela walked slowly back to Lawson's side of the car. The camera followed her. Lawson's window was down and Lomas from the rear seat asked what was happening.

"Well nothing. They said it's not them." Angela sounded genuinely disappointed.

"Of course it's them. They are not going to open up to just anyone," Lomas snapped.

"Show them your D1 security clearance and tell them to speak to Fenton directly in London. They'll have to open up then," David Lawson reassured her.

Angela returned to the intercom beside the gate, her progress shadowed inevitably by the CCTV.

"You again, what now?" the voice demanded, exhibiting signs of growing irritation.

"I have D1 security clearance and I really must speak to your director immediately," Angela insisted. She too was beginning to lose her even manner. She opened out the black wallet which contained her credentials and she held it high, up towards the camera.

"You'll need to hold your hand still, lovey, so I can at least identify the photograph," the voice, now plainly exasperated had become patronising and dismissive.

"Lovey? Listen, mate. You had better get someone down here right now to open up this gate or your life won't be worth living," yelled Angela, instantly incensed by the security man's arrogance.

"Tell your director to get in touch with Sir Geoffrey Fenton in Whitehall on the secure line. All he need say to Sir Geoffrey is Bessomthwaite 288 as a security check. Or of course you could keep me standing here wasting time while the fate of a million people rests in your hands. For God's sake do as I ask and hurry, man, hurry!" she implored.

There was a momentary pause and although his pleasant tone returned, the security man sounded less self assured than before.

"Er, I'll ask," he replied and the intercom clicked off once more.

She walked back to the car. The camera remained stationary as if it had lost interest in her.

"What's the problem?" Lomas snapped again. He was becoming more and more impatient.

"They could be having a cup of tea for all I know. He sounded the type who enjoys the limited powers afforded to him by his minor responsibilities. Bloody idiot," said Angela, still seething from her encounter with the panjandrum behind the gate.

"He's probably waiting for their security to give him authorization to let us through," David Lawson suggested to her. He was increasingly aware of Eric's growing anxiety and, with the Glock still pushed into the back of his neck, was keen to calm the situation as much as possible.

Angela caught his drift and saw then that the man crouched there in the back of the car, usually so cool under pressure, could suddenly unravel. Eric was beginning to get jumpy and venting her frustration wasn't easing the situation in any way.

"Of course they are," she agreed. "So that may take a while I should think. Why don't I go talk to him again, hurry 'em up a bit."

"Get back in the car," Lomas ordered quietly, his voice and manner calm again. "We'll wait. I'm in no hurry."

She did as he asked and they sat in silence for what seemed to her an age.

Lomas had let his hair grow long since he had become non-operational. It suited him she thought. The wind and weather had blown it into a tangle of matted brown curls which hung over his ears and beyond his coat collar. All her life Angela had only ever seen him clean shaven, with short cropped hair. Now, even though his beard appeared to be only a two or three day growth, he had a swarthy unkempt quality about him that again made him very attractive to her; damn him. He had been her first love. As a doe-eyed adolescent she had found her unrequited love for him made all the more painful by his sudden and complete rejection of her. At fourteen this had broken her young heart and later when Eric met and married Katherine all her remaining hopes of a life with him had been expunged.

David Lawson had shown her he was interested and he eventually won her over. There was a certain degree of humanity which David possessed that had been so obviously missing in Eric. It may well have been this ability to remain detached from life which made Lomas such an effective agent, but it was the very lack of it that ultimately made David Lawson so appealing to her and such an ideal lover. She loved him very much and knew that she would eventually have his children and be happy.

Even so she had still hoped secretly she might be the one to, one day, fill the vacuum left in Eric Lomas's life by the deaths of Katherine and his boys. She had always felt a need to defend and protect him from when they were children. This was perhaps the real reason she was there, in the car with a gun hidden up her skirt while he held another to the back of her lover's head. She felt a need to protect him yes, but she knew for certain Eric would not hesitate and kill David without blinking if the situation demanded it. Would she be able to stop him?

Seldom one to ignore the realities of life Angela knew only too well the strains put on them by the work they did, as evidenced by the irascible behaviour of her father. But Eric Lomas was, in her eyes, a special case even so, especially when one considered the personal tragedies he had been forced to endure. Although she was sure David Lawson saw these things in much the same way as she did, she also knew David Lawson's *raison d'etre* was to do his duty. She knew he would do whatever was necessary to defend the country's interests, even if it meant killing Eric to achieve that. She had to prevent this happening too, if she could.

Angela caught herself wondering, if things went badly, which one of these two men would she have to gun down to save the other?

"What are they doing in there?" Angela asked, nervously resetting her mind to the present.

"They are calling London for authorisation I would guess," Lawson reassured her.

"I did tell them to speak to Sir Geoffrey if there was a problem," Angela affirmed.

"That'll please him," David Lawson said. "He thinks we are on our way back."

"What would make him think that?" Lomas enquired, somewhat surprised.

"We had just been recalled, told to return to London, when you hijacked us. Some political pressure from the minister, designed to keep a lid on this and the Americans in the dark as much as possible. Fenton told me the minister wants you dealt with by the police up here, well away from London and that you were to be treated as nothing more than a rogue killer." David Lawson told him. He sounded almost apologetic. "It was you did that copper, in the unmarked Sierra, wasn't it?" he asked.

Lomas nodded. "Yes, a mistake, and I knew it, but he left me little alternative. You know how it can be sometimes."

"I do indeed," Lawson replied. Out of habit he went to feel under his arm for the butt of the Sig that should have been there. He was surprisingly relieved by its absence and the restrictions this would impose on any action he could take against Eric.

"Easy fella," warned Lomas, spotting the slight movement of Lawson's right hand. "Keep both your hands on the wheel."

"And the American, the CIA man in Baghdad? Were we right to assume that was you too?" Angela asked to redirect his attention.

"Yes, me again I'm afraid, but for Queen and Country this time. I am pretty sure he guessed I had found something quite important in the desert. He confronted me with it over dinner that night and wanted answers but by then I was beginning to understand the greater implications my discovery would have if it were to become more widely known exactly what I had found and where. Difficult for the prime minister then to stand up in the house and tell parliament there is definitive proof of the existence of chemical weapons in Iraq without admitting our previous involvement in the supply. And if the Americans were to find out, even now, they'll force his hand and it will be the war Britain has been trying to avoid for the last ten years. So best we kept this to ourselves I would have thought. Of course this also helps place me in a good position to negotiate my exit strategy."

"I get your point," said Lawson. "The minister on the other hand appears not to agree, he called in the locals; it wasn't Fenton. He wanted you dealt with by me."

"Well still looks like he could get his wish."

"Not really, not now he knows she is here," said Lawson, pointing out Angela's unplanned involvement.

"Oh I see, just a passenger then," Lomas taunted.

"He will want her back safe, no matter what. He'll throw everything at you now."

"Good, they can't ignore me now and the more fuss he tries to make only makes my bargaining position even stronger."

"You do have an escape plan then?" Angela asked him, spitefully returning his jibe.

"Not one that involved the two of you. No. Although you do appear to have turned the odds somewhat in my favour, wouldn't you say? Ah well, around such small things our lives revolve," Lomas mused.

Chapter Eighteen

Fate and Small Things

A green light on Fenton's telephone flashed accompanied by a muffled buzz.

"Yes, Fiona," he said, lifting the receiver. He listened for a moment then replied. "You'd better put them through; it may be something from Lawson."

He pressed a button beneath the flashing light and a man's voice came loudly from the speaker.

"Sir Geoffrey?"

"Yes, what is it?"

"This is Professor Rutherford," said a metallic voice from the telephone. "I am the new CEO of Biotech Life Sciences in Cumbria."

"Congratulations. You have a problem I understand."

"We do indeed have a problem, Sir Geoffrey."

"Well get on with it then man, what is it, this problem?" Sir Geoffrey asked, impatiently.

"I have been advised by my security people that one of your agents, a woman with two unidentified men, is in a car at our perimeter gate and demanding entry. The woman has D1 security clearance and stressed the importance of their immediate access to our establishment."

"Then do just that; allow them immediate access." With this stern response he aimed to stress a great urgency. It was obvious to Fenton right away that two of the group were surely

212

Lawson and Angela. The third he hoped would prove to be Lomas.

"She told our security I was to give you a code word and some numbers as verification; Bessomthwaite, followed by these numbers: two, eight, eight. She said you'd know what they meant."

Of course Fenton thought he knew what they meant. He thought they meant Lawson had tracked Eric down and probably had him in the car, alive. The two vials of 288 had been recovered and David Lawson had brought them to the most secure location he could possibly have found to dispose of them. Well done Duffy, Fenton allowed himself a smile, well done.

"You must allow them access to all areas and unimpeded access at that. Wherever they need to go, do you understand me? My authority comes from the very highest level and I expect you to comply immediately and completely with this instruction. Have I made myself clear?" he commanded.

"You have, perfectly," the professor replied. "But I can't just..." he began but Fenton curtly interrupted him.

"They are highly trained armed security officers with a prisoner. Leave everything to us and keep your people well out of their way. You are to offer them no hindrance whatsoever, we don't want any unfortunate accidents. I shall arrange for their onward transportation, just keep them secure for now. All you need do is to contain them for the next few hours and I will coordinate the extraction operation personally from here."

Sir Geoffrey closed the line abruptly, not allowing the professor time to offer any objections.

"Fiona," he called into the telephone.

"Yes, sir?"

"Get me Special Branch will you please, on a closed line. I want Commander Lockwood, not one of his bloody assistants."

"Yes, sir, right away."

He and Harry Lockwood, both consultants to the Cobra panel, quickly agreed on a plan. They had worked together before on several security operations and had an unspoken respect for each other. Fenton felt confident that the threat to the country from a weapon of mass destruction was shortly to be extinguished and that his little angel would soon be returned to him unharmed. The end game to this latest round of '*catch as catch can*' with General Hassan was yet to be played out it was true but as he replaced the telephone he did wonder if these unfolding events, over which he had no real control, would prove his confidence justified.

It had been a long day already and he had not eaten. So he decided as there was little more he could do from his desk he should walk to his club and take a late luncheon. He wanted to allow himself a moment or two to relish the frisson of relief he was feeling. As he put on his scarf and overcoat he smiled with the anticipation of roast beef and a glass of fine claret. Lawson could handle the situation up there with Eric; he had no doubts. The genie, he believed, was back in the bottle and plans were in place to quietly put the stopper back in it. It was out of his hands now. All he could do now was to wait and hope for the best outcome. Fenton had rarely found himself in this position and he did not like it one bit.

Professor Rutherford was left less than impressed too with the situation in which Sir Geoffrey had left him. He was forced to call a meeting of all his staff to appraise them of the unusual circumstances, which meant interrupting their work.

He informed them they were to expect three important visitors. They were to allow the visitors freedom to go wherever they wished, whilst observing all the routine and required information containment procedures used for any of the dangerous materials they might be asked about. He advised them to go about their work as normally as they could, but to avoid any unnecessary contact with their guests.

"However," he added, "I want one of you to act as liaison and accompany them while they are here. I would do this myself of course, but I have to be on hand if Whitehall should call us again with instructions. Any volunteers?"

Martin Frazier would not have been able to tell you exactly why he stood forward with his hand in the air. He had never volunteered for anything in his life before and with good reason.

As well as a masters degree in both chemistry and biology from Edinburgh he could also boast a first with honours in mathematics from Oxford as his first degree; this he received when he was just fourteen-years-old. Now, at the age of thirty, he understood very well there were no favourable percentages in volunteering. In almost every instance in history it is always the volunteers who fall by the wayside while the folk who keep their heads down endure. Historically the odds did not ever seem to be in favour of the volunteer.

He had intended to impress the new graduate chemist he had his eye on but she seemed singularly unimpressed by his bold gesture. Had he known the fate that awaited him at the Barrow Beck gate Martin might well have had second thoughts.

Escort three VIPs around, what's the worst that can happen, he had asked himself.

Our lives are indeed changed by such small things, and fate is no more than a string of unforeseen coincidences.

Chapter Nineteen

Under Benlow's Fell

A tense silence that fed on Angela's sanity seemed to fill the car around her. It nibbled on her fears leaving her only crumbs of confidence to sift through. *I must hold it all together* she told herself, keep strong and focused.

"What are you planning to do in there Eric?" she asked him suddenly, regaining her self-belief. She nodded towards the gate.

"Do you know, now I am here I am not certain. When I left Iraq my intentions were clear to me and justified. But now…" His voice tailed off into silence. Lomas leaned forward and placed his free hand on Angela's shoulder. "I have no desire to harm either of you. Providing you both do exactly as I ask, we can all walk away from this," he reassured her.

"You still have the Bessomthwaite 288 with you I imagine?" David Lawson ventured.

"I do. That's why we're here. It has been my intention since leaving Weymouth to release the spores I have with me into the central air-conditioning system of this palace of contagion," he confessed. "They will have installed highly sensitive detectors that should trigger their alarm system and initiate an evacuation procedure followed by a total lock-down. With any luck, there will be no casualties. Then, owing to the type and level of the contamination, the whole facility will be unable to function for at least a decade or more and this inhumane research will have to be halted."

"A protest action then," Angela summarised.

"If you like," Lomas conceded.

"That doesn't sound too unreasonable, does it, David?" she asked.

"A bloody dangerous protest," Lawson suggested.

"A small price to pay I believe if it prevents the continuation of this abominable research." His passion was cold and calculated. "You do know the true nature of their research here?"

"Yes, I do, of course I do. They work on producing antidotes to counteract any threat from the work Russia and other countries that still fund this particular field of bio-technology," Lawson answered. "I've read some of the files."

"A little naïve, David, but understand you've only read the files Fenton wants you to read, have no doubt. He has a limited regard for the whole truth of things. That's how he motivates people. The world should be shown what these weapons can do and could do, in the wrong hands. Then perhaps someone with sufficient power and influence will say enough is enough. Before it is too late, before chemistry is developed over which we no longer have control. Until now we have been careering headlong towards the real possibility of unintentionally destroying all human life on this planet. My intention is to slow down this driverless train long enough for governments to realise where it is heading.

"None of this material is supposed to exist you know." Lomas continued. "All biological and chemical weapons development was supposed to have stopped in the eighties. There was a moratorium agreed at the UN. All the NATO countries and the Warsaw Pact, who signed up, and China too, would halt production and development of all chemical and biological weaponry. Did they? No, they all just carried on as before, only more secretively that's all. The Russians carried on their research with barely a pause. So the Americans, who were vocally unenthusiastic about the whole arrangement from the beginning, had to at least match Russian progress in the field. Nothing changed. And of course, we Brits not wanting to be left behind jumped straight back on the train too. Only thing is now, having lost morality as its driver, the train is hurtling even faster towards its own destruction and ours along with it. Each new venomous concoction is parried by a new anti-venom; each manufactured plague is countered by cultivated antibiotics, every toxic chemical made harmless by some cleverly devised antidote, in a never ending and terrifying contest."

"There is no way you can be sure there will be no casualties, no collateral damage, caused by your plan either, can you?" David pointed out.

"There can be no certainty of that, none at all, but this madness has to be stopped, at least long enough for these people to come to their senses. Otherwise we all ride on with them towards our annihilation, which will come one day. It will come when no antidote can be found, or an antibiotic becomes resistant, or the latest anti-venom proves to be ineffective," said Lomas.

"Do you know I found Bessomthwaite 288 in a tin shed in Iraq?" he said with quiet anger obvious in his voice. "You do realise what that means?"

Lawson and Angela remained silent, waiting for the storm to pass. They looked at each other once, quickly, just a glance but enough for them to agree that now was not the time to challenge Lomas or his philosophy.

"It means," Lomas continued, "someone in Whitehall would have had to give permission for its exportation. We gave, or more likely sold, this material to Saddam Hussein. He was at war with Iran at the time probably, so our government assisted him. He seemed to be on our side then remember, not considered to be any kind of threat at all. However, what the minister of the day failed to appreciate was the scale by which this particular microbe could be dangerous to human health. Or perhaps he did appreciate it but felt that as long as Arabs were killing Arabs we should help out. After all is said and done, at least they were not killing us. So the degree by which, and the speed with which this substance was able spread its contagion would have been of little concern to him. Those voices, you can hear them along the corridors of power even now; haunting us still. Right here at this very place our research continues secretly, developing new ways of inflicting destruction not just on our enemies but on the innocent too. I have promised myself, in the names of my dead sons, to stop what goes on here. Then perhaps those with the power to bring this train to a halt will stop and take a long hard look at where we were going. If I perish, if we perish, if half a million perish along with us, I agree it would indeed be unfortunate and yet may serve to emphasise my point to an even wider audience. But stopped it must be, here, today." Lomas fell silent.

Without warning the metal gate began to slide slowly sideways and retract into the grey steel pillar to their right. The CCTV camera resumed its monitoring of the car as it progressed and they passed beyond the opened portal.

Lawson drove slowly along a narrow concrete roadway which passed between tall pines. The closely planted trees pressed in over the road from both sides. This and the ever narrowing ribbon of blue sky above the tree-line seemed to gradually suck the light from around the car. Lawson turned on the car's headlights and proceeded until finally there was no blue above them and the sky had disappeared beneath a low concrete ceiling. They were driving into a sparsely lit tunnel heading down under the fell, into the heart of the mountain.

At first, Martin Frazier could not believe his luck. From inside Biotech's main reception area, a sealed, triple-glazed booth in the underground loading bay, he watched the car draw slowly to a halt. He watched as a short and perfectly formed young blonde woman stepped out from the car; her eyes were warm and friendly. She wore a light brown, well made, close fitting business suit with a knee length skirt. The open collared white shirt underneath her jacket showed the merest suggestion of an ample cleavage. *Your percentages are starting to improve*, thought Martin. He raised a welcoming hand to her and she responded in kind. *Play your cards right, Martin, you could be in here, son.* Sadly, this delusion proved to be short lived. As the two men who were with her got out of the car and stood beside her, his momentary romance with her was cruelly crushed.

One man, whom he guessed had been the driver, left the car by the passenger door as the young blonde woman had done; the door nearest to Martin. He must have shuffled across from the driver's side to get out. This man was tall, slim and broad across the shoulders. His eyes were fierce and bright.

The second man then got out from the nearside too, but he used the rear door. He was shorter and wider and seemed more compact than his companion but it was difficult to assess his true form, concealed as it was beneath a massively oversized greatcoat. His eyes were piercing and as cold as steel; a killer's eyes, Martin concluded. This man looked as though he needed a good wash and clean clothes. He was muddy and his hair matted with rain and grime.

Both men exuded a confidence that only comes from knowing one can handle oneself well. These were men not to be messed with, that was patently obvious. Martin did not possess their brand of confidence in any measurable quantity and his previous bravado, which had already begun to collapse like a springtime snowman, melted still further when he spotted the smaller man was holding a gun. At that point his anal sphincter nearly let him down. He saw the smaller man with the gun say something to the other two and they moved forward towards Martin's cabin. *Oh my God, I'm gonna fill my pants,* he thought.

"You both know my capabilities." Lomas warned them, "You make one move I haven't asked you to make, either of you, and I'll drop you where you stand. Do I make myself clear?"

Lawson nodded. Angela nodded, but suspected he might have difficulty despatching her without any hesitation.

"Now move." This was his first instruction and they moved.

"Oh good," said Lomas, noticing Martin Frazier with his spotless white lab coat and terrified expression. "Looks like we have a welcoming committee. Open the fucking door, Sparky," he shouted at Martin through the glass.

Martin obeyed the instruction without comment, quickly punching numbers into a keypad beside the entrance. The glass panel slid noiselessly open and the three visitors stepped inside.

"I have to close the door again, sir," said Martin nervously. "Security," he added, needlessly.

"Go ahead, but no surprises, Sparky, please, I'm a little jumpy today." Lomas waved his empty hand towards the door, but the gun in the other hand remained steady and aimed between the backs of his two colleagues.

Martin punched some keys on the pad and the door closed. He led the group across the reception area where he punched some more numbers into another keypad and the wall itself swung away from him into a corridor of spotlessly clean stainless steel. The door behind them shut automatically with a dull resounding clunk followed by a faint hiss. The short corridor closed at its opposing end by yet another shining metal door provided a sealed airlock from the world outside. They were now securely contained inside the facility while the rest of the planet remained safe from all the plagues and pestilences stored there, beneath Benlow's Fell.

Martin keyed in the code and with a long gasp the door before him slid aside leading into a high open chasm. They followed Martin into this huge space until they were standing in what seemed to be the middle of the inside of a massive stainless steel dome.

Surrounding this wide area were several individual and self-contained laboratory units each encased by thick triple glazed panels and more spotlessly clean stainless steel. It was as if they had walked into a silver-lined cavern; a bright and shining cathedral of homage to the God of science and cleanliness.

"Hey, Sparky," Lomas called out. "Where exactly are we?"

"In relation to what exactly?" Martin replied. "I need the question to be a little more specific to give you the most accurate answer."

"Ah, a bright lad I see. What is your name, young man?" Lomas asked the thirty-year-old bio-chemist.

"Martin," said Martin.

"Well, Martin, exactly where are we in relation to the rest of this facility?" clarified Lomas.

"We are, sir, in the very centre of things right here. Around us are our laboratories. There are six main laboratories, as you can see. Each is separated from the others by a vacuum to nullify the chances of cross contamination from its neighbours of course."

"Of course," said Lomas, sarcastically.

"Each lab is developing its own specific research, you understand. Projects can vary from micro-biology and genetics, to chemical compound research and development: in broad terms that is,"

Martin continued.

"Then there are the two upper floors which are outside the seal of this one, the primary self-contained area. First floor is mainly dedicated to storage of sterile equipment, and kitchen facilities of course. We have to eat after all."

Lomas found he was about to say 'Of course' once more but stopped himself.

"And the second floor is the administration offices and our toilets and shower rooms," Martin said in conclusion.

"What about de-contamination, you must have an area for that, surely," Lomas asked.

"Well of course," Martin replied indignantly. "We have just passed through it in fact. That hissing sound you heard was the release of a cocktail of colourless, odourless gases developed here as a by-product of some research I did last year. We haven't found a bug yet that is resistant to it." Martin divulged this secret with some pride.

"Well done, Sparky; you are a clever old thing and no mistake," Lomas remarked. "However, I have here a bug of sorts that might give your cleansing gases a run for their money." He plunged his gun-free hand into the pocket of his coat and drew from it the small vial of magenta liquid he had concealed there and held it up to the light.

"Bessomthwaite 288," Martin marvelled. "Is that it?"

He had recognised it immediately.

"It is indeed, Martin."

Angela and David Lawson turned to see what it was that Lomas was holding high in the air, upwards towards the ceiling.

"Careful the two of you, my promise still stands. I'll drop you without a moment's thought."

"Those big fans up there, Martin, do they filter to the outside?" Lomas asked, whilst still keeping a wary eye on his two companions for any sudden movements.

"No, not at all. This chamber is a self-contained sealed unit. The air is drawn up by the fans where it gets filtered through various compounds we have developed. It is cooled and then it gets recycled. Under normal working they are only on minimum power and merely assist the natural convective effect created by a space of this shape. That is to say the warm dirty air rises and the cleaned cold air sinks back down around the outer skin of the dome to be re-introduced at floor level through those ducts you see on the wall all the way round." Martin knew his stuff.

"What would happen if I released the contents of this in here? Could any of it escape into the outside atmosphere?" Lomas asked.

"I'd say it was impossible," replied Martin, emphatically.

"Then that, Sparky, is good enough for me."

"But this whole area, including the labs, would be out of action for months, years probably," Martin warned him.

"Outstanding!" Lomas smiled for the first time since he had left France. "Okay, Sparky, you're the chap for me. Now what I want you to do first of all is to remove your tie and bind these two with it, back to back, and on their knees. Clear?"

Martin immediately began struggling to undo his tie and did not bother with any kind of reply. The knot, which he had tied quickly only ten minutes before when he had volunteered for his current duties, obstinately refused to loosen.

"You two, on your knees, back to back, legs apart. You know the drill." Lomas waved the gun and took a step towards Lawson and Angela. They dropped to their knees and Martin who, having mercifully managed to free himself from his tie, bound their wrists tightly together with it, under Eric's watchful supervision.

"That's good. Now, Sparky, I will explain your role in this. You are my hostage and as my hostage you are in a situation of total safety or certain death; which of these will depend entirely on your ability, the three of you, to follow instructions. If you do as I ask, you will give me no reason to shoot you. These two people are my friends Martin. We work together defending this country from its enemies. They are my family and as such I am unlikely to shoot either one of them. But if they do not follow my instructions I will shoot you and they know I will do it. Do you both understand me?" Lomas addressed this question to his two captives. Neither answered, but both nodded.

"They understand, Martin, do you see? They understand, so you are safe. Now I require from you the codes you used to open those doors. Give them to me and you remain, safe," Lomas threatened.

Martin answered without hesitation, "My name. Today's code is my name."

"Not Sparky?" asked Lomas, and chuckled impishly.

"No, not Martin either. It's the letters that spell out the phrase 'My Name' expressed as numbers."

"Which numbers?" Lomas asked, sounding less self-assured.

"Those that correspond to each letter's position in the Roman alphabet," Martin explained. "Today the numbers are: thirteen, twenty-five, fourteen, one, thirteen and five. So the sequence of: 1325141135 will open the door."

"Both doors?"

"Yes, all doors," Martin replied with an expansive gesture of his hands.

"Good lad. Now, I need a telephone, I must speak to Sir Geoffrey in London. Can you find one for me?" Lomas asked.

"There are intercoms in each of the labs where you can get an outside line," said Martin with a more confident air.

"Are they open?"

Lawson had been fiddling with the binding restraining him and Angela, but Martin seemed to have done a more than adequate job on them. Angela, however, felt hers loosen a little and tapped Lawson's ankle with her hand. He got the message.

"Lab One is vacant at the moment. There are seldom any projects conducted in there. We use it mainly as a back-up if we have a problem in one of the other five. It is the only lab with access to the other levels via its own secure vacuum seal. Like the one we have just used it also has its own de-contamination vault."

"Open it."

Holding the vial of Bessomthwaite 288 in one hand and the Glock 17 in his other, Lomas ushered Lawson and Angela to their feet and side stepped them through the opened door and into Lab One. Martin followed, leaving the door behind them open and unlocked, on Eric's instruction. He handed the magenta vial to Martin, for safe keeping. Martin held it in both hands and stared at it as if it would explode any second. Lomas removed the wired handset from the holster on the wall and listened; nothing.

"Press nine for a line," said Martin. "Or hold and Sophie will ask what connection you want."

Immediately the pleasant voice of a woman spoke in Eric's ear and apologised for her delayed response. She had been advised by the director to accede to any request their important guests might wish to make.

"How may I be of assistance Sir?" she asked him warmly.

In that brief moment, Eric's attention was diverted enough for Angela to free one hand, reach up under her skirt and draw out a small pistol from where it had been strapped to the inside of her upper thigh. She had concealed it there that morning, before she left London: just to be on the safe side. She realised Eric no longer held the balance of power. It was Martin who held the deadly vial. Twisting her other hand free she cocked the gun but Lawson lunged at her to knock her sideways. Even so she managed to fire off three shots in rapid succession before the gun clicked and jammed.

Lomas fell backwards out of the open doorway into the atrium and rolled over. He had been hit and was not moving.

Angela held the small Beretta out in front of her for a long moment but gradually lowered the gun, unsure what to do next. She turned to Lawson, who was struggling to release himself from his bonds. As he struggled to free his hands and arms he raised them high in the air to show Lomas he was unarmed.

Angela stared at Lawson and such anger welled up in her that for that one second, she was ugly.

"Why? Why the hell did you shove me over?" she begged him to tell her.

He nodded for her to turn round and face the open door where Lomas was already up and in the doorway on one knee pointing the Glock at them both. A single bullet had passed through the left sleeve of his greatcoat but he had remained uninjured.

"To stop you from killing your own brother," Lomas answered for him. "Well half brother actually. I guess Fenton told him the family secret but kept you in the dark. It is for that reason alone you are not laying dead on the floor yourself, sister." Lomas spat out the words.

Chapter Twenty

Useful Dead

Those pieces of her life that had never fitted properly before now suddenly clicked into place. Shock and disbelief travelled with equal speed through Angela's mind and showed themselves in the expression on her face. Some of the natural colour in her cheeks faded too as she finally grasped the implications of what had just happened.

It was perhaps not the best time to examine her feelings regarding how this new knowledge was going to alter her life and her future. She was brought to the realisation, that it would be much better for her to let the questions wait for now, by the quickly developing situation she saw now in front of her.

"Help me! Please, someone." It was Martin who pleaded with them, anyone of them would have done. He had taken two bullets from Angela's gun and for him any future was optimistic. His life was ending, although he had not yet realised it.

"I seem to have sustained an injury," he added unnecessarily.

He looked down at the shattered pens in his left breast pocket and at the growing rosette of his bright red arterial blood widening beneath it and staining his immaculate white lab coat. He dropped to his knees, still holding the magenta vial of Bessomthwaite 288 in one slightly shaky hand. He attempted to speak again, to make any kind of sound, but nothing would come from his gasping goldfish mouth.

Lomas relieved him of the magenta vial as he slumped forward slowly onto his face. The two bullets from Angela's gun had penetrated his thoracic cavity, one pierced the aorta, and the other had entered his right lung. He was slowly drowning in his own blood.

"Nice shooting, sis," mocked Lomas. They watched as the pool of blood made a sudden surge as the muscles in Martin's body began to relax and his death rapidly approached. Lomas stepped back a bit to avoid getting any on his shoes.

"You're an animal." Angela spat the words back at him.

"I am what our father has made me. Now slide the gun over," Lomas snapped back.

She complied by kicking it across the floor to him.

Lomas stooped and picked it up. He released the magazine onto the floor and took a long look at the empty gun. The small gun was warm in his hand where the metal had held onto her body heat. He smiled to himself. Most definitely a lady's pistol he thought as he tossed it far into the atrium.

Stepping forward he stood beside Lawson, ignoring her completely. He spoke quietly into Lawson's ear giving him instructions.

"Yes, I will do that, Eric. You can rely on me," David Lawson assured him. "But your father, I won't be able to prevent him trying to take you when you are out of here?"

"Just deliver the message and make certain he understands that he will never find it if he or anyone else comes for me. Is that clear?"

"As crystal," Lawson replied.

Angela watched in horror as the red puddle around Martin's motionless body grew larger. "What about us?" she asked, hopeful it was not to be her last ever question.

"You'll both be safe in here. You know the code for the doors. I am going through this way and driving out the way we came in, but you should be sensible now and not follow me. It will be fatal if you do. Use that one." He pointed to the airlock in the opposite wall.

Lawson and Angela turned and saw a keypad beside the stainless steel door which would lead them to their escape and safety. When Angela turned back he had gone.

The door had closed on behind Lomas with a soft swoosh and they saw him in the atrium by the exit airlock holding the vial of Bessomthwaite 288 high above his head.

He nodded to Lawson who then recovered the dangling hand set which Lomas had dropped when Angela had shot at him. He held the phone up to the glass so Lomas could see it.

Lomas punched numbers into the keypad and his door to the outside slid open. David Lawson spoke into the phone.

"Sophie, are you still there?" Lawson asked.

"I am."

She had heard the shots but was calmer now and remained professional. "How may I be of assistance, Sir?" she asked, repeating her earlier question to Lomas.

"To start with you can get Sir Geoffrey Fenton on the line for me. If he is not in his office, at this time of day you should try his club. It is rather important I speak with him as soon as possible, as you no doubt appreciate," Lomas replied.

"I do indeed, but give me a moment." She responded calmly.

The seconds passed into minutes and after what seemed like an age Fenton's voice was in his ear. He raised his hand to Lomas as a 'thumbs up' and with a most uncharacteristically flamboyant sweep of the arm that would not have looked out of place in a rock guitar riff, Eric smashed the glass vial into the floor.

Then he was gone. The stainless steel door slid shut and Lomas disappeared from their lives forever.

* * *

"What the blazes! Careful what you say, Lawson, Rutherford is on the line too, you know," said Fenton, still believing the situation was recoverable.

"Sir Geoffrey, it's gone far beyond that now. Before I explain, if you have Special Branch or any of the others outside you must tell them immediately to stand down. And we must get word to the gate here straightaway to let his car pass unhindered. Is Professor Rutherford able to do that?"

"Yes he is," Professor Rutherford interjected. "I'll arrange for that to happen right away." He was as anxious as anyone for things to quickly return to normal, but he was in for a big surprise in that regard.

Through the sealed glass windows of Lab One Lawson could see pieces of the smashed glass vial and the puddle of magenta liquid spread out on the floor of the atrium. A faint pink vapour had begun to rise as the magenta liquid evaporated. He followed its slow rise, drawn up by convection, as Martin had said, towards the sensors in the domed roof and the whirling fans that would eventually distribute the noisome, noxious gas through the whole area. Sirens began to sound loudly and persistently. He could see the fans already beginning to spin faster. How quickly the movement of their blades became just a blur.

"Sir Geoffrey, I am going to speak to you from somewhere less exposed," Lawson told him.

"Angela and I need to leave where we are rather quickly now but listen. Eric still has one of the vials hidden somewhere safe. Tell the troops to let him pass or we'll never find it. I'll explain everything to you when we are outside and safe."

Fenton spoke and Lawson answered. "Yes, a bit shaken but she's fine, sir." He replaced the receiver.

Lawson grabbed Angela's arm and pulled her away from Martin's lifeless body.

"Come on, Daddy wants a word with you," he told her.

"I have a few questions for him too," she replied.

Lawson was punching numbers into the keypad but nothing was happening. In his haste he must have missed one but he could hardly ask Martin to remind him of the sequence.

Angela looked back at Martin's corpse. It was lying flat out on the floor with its arms at its sides just as it had fallen; head facing towards them, eyes rolled back, lids half closed, its lifeblood spread out both sides like a pair of crimson wings.

"We can't just leave him there like that, David," Angela insisted.

"Martin is surely dead, but that doesn't mean he can't still be of assistance to us," Lawson said to himself.

"Cover his head then," he told Angela, taking off his jacket and handing it to her. "It will serve us best to leave the body where it is. Even though he is dead, young Sparky there could yet have one final function to perform."

Angela placed David's jacket across the shoulders of the dead body, covering its face and eyes.

"What possible use can he be to anyone any more?" Angela asked, her voice full of remorse.

In the atrium the cloud of pink mist continued to climb up into the roof fans. Lawson attempted to punch correct numbers into the keypad again. This time the metal door did slide open with a reassuring hiss from the airlock.

"I'll tell you later. Now come on and hurry. We have to get out of here now or we'll be contaminated and dead ourselves," Lawson warned and with some urgency.

Fenton sat in a high backed winged armchair. The other chairs and chesterfields in the sitting room were upholstered in the same luxuriously soft dull mustard coloured leather. Low tables, fashioned from the darkest South American mahogany, ornately carved and gleaming with a patina only a century of polishing could achieve, were placed between each group of seats and sofas. Rising up from the hearth of a large fireplace at the farthest end of the room the flames of a freshly stoked fire licked at the black bricks of the old chimney. He watched the yellow flames flicker through the nut brown liquid in a tall thin glass of amaretto he was holding up before taking another sip. The thick almond flavoured liqueur, which held in long sticky rivulets to the inside of the glass, glinted with the fire's golden light. Although it had been mild outside of late, a backing easterly wind had brought a chilly squall of rain along the Thames that afternoon and he had arrived cold and wet at his club in Whitehall. So he had, immediately on his arrival, asked the steward to make up the sitting room fire for after his luncheon.

Owing to the telephone conversation earlier with Professor Rutherford at Biotech he had begun his lunch later than usual, but in high spirits. It had appeared then that Lawson had the situation well in hand. His darling daughter was safe, there was a good chance Eric could be brought back into the fold and an embarrassing public enquiry would be avoided; assuming of course the Bessomthwaite 288 was safely contained within Biotech's airtight facility.

He had enjoyed his lunch, its lateness giving it extra flavour, and dessert was rhubarb and ginger crumble with the tinned custard he loved so much. In fact, he had been scraping the spoon around the bowl to savour every last scrap of it when the steward had brought a telephone to his table.

"Sorry to disturb your lunch, Sir Geoffrey. Major Lawson for you, sir: sounds urgent."

He had listened in disbelief to what Lawson was telling him.

"But is she all right?" he had asked before Lawson needed to go.

Fenton had immediately telephoned Commander Lockwood there, at the dining table, such was the imperative for a swift change of plan. Lockwood had agreed with Fenton's assessment of the situation and acceding to Sir Geoffrey's request, stood down his team.

Now the lovely food he had only just eaten was turning to acid in his stomach and the amaretto burned like fire in his belly. His daughter was safe and Lawson too, but he saw few other positives to be gleaned from the position in which he was now placed.

When Lawson had phoned back and explained the full extent of the damage Eric had managed to cause, it seemed clear to Fenton his own position had become rather precarious.

They had one man dead which, in other circumstances, would have been considered acceptable if the dead man had not been shot by Fenton's own daughter. She should not have been there in the first place but he would try to protect her from a full scale enquiry of course. Although how effective he could be after this he was still unsure.

Eric, who by now would have disappeared again, still had a vial of Bessomthwaite 288 hidden; God knows where. By announcing he would be retiring with immediate effect and threatening to present himself to the Americans directly if any attempt was made to hunt him down, Lomas had effectively left Fenton with little option but to submit to this *coup de grâce*.

However, Fenton realised all of these things could have been contained with very little fallout coming in his direction if it had not been for the level of contamination at Biotech Life Sciences. All its research would have to be shut down for the foreseeable future and that was the real cruncher. The minister was unlikely to volunteer to take any responsibility and would attempt to protect the PM from any involvement if the Americans got wind of what had happened. Fenton knew he would have to resign or he would be retired.

There had been whispers that a woman would replace him if he was ever to retire; MI6 had one. Fenton smiled at the thought.

Good God, what a mess. As he sat staring into the flames, he had to concede that it had been his responsibility alone to clear up the mess and he had failed. He began to understand the true enormity of the dilemma which the PM would now have to face as a result of this failure. The government would survive and so would the PM, probably. The prime minister was a good man and with his powerful gift for oratory he could no doubt persuade parliament and the country to go with him.

His own position Fenton saw as quite untenable. An illustrious career brought to an end and laid low by an organism so small you could fit millions on a pin head. Still, he'd had a good run and now he could spend *all* his time tending to his roses.

Bessomthwaite Two Eight Eight, even the sound of the words gave him dyspepsia. He drained his glass, but immediately regretted it.

Chapter Twenty One

Epilogue

"Have you read the English papers today?"

"No! Are they filled with good news?"

"Not exactly, I'll read you a small article from page five of the *London Telegraph* shall I?" The telephone line between them crackled and she asked, "Are you still there?"

"I am. Please, continue."

"'The company Biotech Life Sciences has been forced to close one of its laboratories near Keswick. It has been announced by the Home Office today that due to technical difficulties at their plant in Cumbria all operations there have been suspended for the foreseeable future. A spokesman for the company assured our reporter that there is no risk to the surrounding area or the local population and that there was definitely no truth in the rumours generated by animal rights activists that the closure is due to pressure exerted by their demonstrations and the support of the wider public for their cause. However, a source at the Home Office has suggested that in recognising a growing concern nationwide regarding GM crops, which is the main component of Biotech Life Sciences' research, the Government has decided to review the range of licences it grants the company to carry out this research.'"

"You must know what that means?" she asked.

"I do. It means later today the Prime Minister of Great Britain will be making a statement in the House of Commons saying Weapons of Mass Destruction exist in Iraq and that Britain must join the Americans and prepare for war."

"Then you have heard. So our plan has worked then, General?"

"It has indeed. Lomas must have released the stuff in the only place it could do the least damage and yet have maximum effect, and still we have the result we were hoping for. No massive outbreak or death toll but one can't expect to get everything one desires for so little investment. This is more than enough. Well done, my dear, well done." The general was quite emotional at the prospect of preparing a suitable welcome for his eagerly anticipated visitors.

"And how may I reward you, my dear, for your role in this subterfuge?" he asked.

"You should give me back my brother, as we agreed," advised the woman.

"I shall honour our agreement, as promised," the general assured her.

"Wait, I'll bet you have not heard the best bit yet."

"Pray enlighten me then."

"Third page of *The New York Times*," she began.

"My, you have been thorough."

"It's my nursing training. It teaches one to be precise and it is in a good cause I hope?"

"Get on with it," demanded the general, becoming suddenly impatient as if someone else had just stepped into his office.

"It's only two paragraphs. They read: 'A spokesman for the Central Intelligence Agency gave a short press conference at its headquarters in Langley today. He stated that information received from their counterparts in London, indicates that the man found dead on the moors in Cumbria, England was the person being sought in connection with the suspicious death of a minor US Government official in Baghdad last month. The agency therefore is closing down any further investigations into this tragic death.

The US Government has expressed its relief that an event which could have soured relations between Washington and London has been resolved.' Well? You did not know that did you General? So I guess that's Lomas out of the way too and normal service between Washington and London has been resumed."

"No! You are right, I did not know that."

"They are coming, General. Sir Geoffrey can't keep a lid on this now. The British and the Americans are coming just as you planned."

"As Allah has decreed," corrected the general. "Thank you for your help and I am pleased to tell you your brother is on his way to you. The ink is not yet dry on his release papers."

"Then merci, General, and au revoir," she replied and switched off her phone.

"It has been a pleasure, Fabien," he said to dead air. He replaced the receiver in its cradle on his desk and turned to the old friend who had just entered the office.

"Are they coming, General?" asked the friend.

"Soon! The Americans are coming soon," the general replied. "We must prepare."

"I'll warn Mundai. And the British, what of the British effendi?"

"They are coming too, Khalid. They will rid us of the crazy one," promised the general.

General Mahmud Hassan al Majid held a fond regard for the British and for the English particularly. "Always liked a good war have the British," he added, wistfully.

* * *

Fabien Neuville put her phone down on the dresser next to her big comfortable bed. She lay back onto the pillows and stretched her bare arms above her head and breathed a long deep sigh as the newspapers slipped from the covers onto the floor. It was less a sigh of frustration and more a sigh that signified great relief.

"Francoise is coming home."

She breathed the words softly, as if to herself. "He'll be here tomorrow or the day after I should think."

"I am glad you are so happy," said her companion, who lay on the bed next to her. Like her, her lover was as naked as the day he was born.

Fabien rolled over so her body pressed along the length of him. He closed his eyes and felt a soft gentle hand, slowly, gently, stroke his face.

"You should keep the beard," she said, feeling the stiff bristly hair around his mouth. "I like it. It tickles me."

"You are without shame, ma'am, and you a nurse and all." He was mocking her slightly, but he didn't necessarily want her to stop. She felt warm and wanton, squeezed against him as she was.

"We are the worst, us nurses you know," she assured him. "Now, Mr Lomas, are you ready for your treatment?"

He opened his eyes and smiled into her loving, lovely face.

"First I must phone Sir Geoffrey," Lomas said. "He has kept his end of the bargain. I have to keep my part of it and tell him where I buried the camera."

"The camera? Why the camera?" asked Fabien, puzzled.

"The second vial of Bessomthwaite 288 is still in the battery compartment."

"No wonder I couldn't find them when I searched your stuff when you first arrived," Fabien admitted.

"What! You went through my things?" Lomas was stunned.

"Of course. The general wanted to be sure you still had the vials with you."

"I'm not sure I like the idea of you going through my things."

"Is that so?" she purred at him and rolled onto her back, putting her hands behind her head and so exposing him all her nakedness. "I'll let you go through all my things."

"You are brazen, brazen I tell you," he said, forgiving her instantly.

He leant across her body and felt her nipples hard against his chest as he picked up her phone and pressed the numbers for Fenton's private phone.

"I'll deal with you, young lady, in just a moment," he promised.

"It had better take longer than that," she whispered.

They waited for the connection and for Fenton to answer but she could not help touching him, to reassure herself that he was real and really there. She felt him tremor at her touch.

"Where *did* you bury the camera?" she asked.

"I shan't tell you. Be patient, you'll hear."

She prodded him under the ribs with a slender finger.

"All right. Let's just say, Mother is taking care of it."